ASHMORE PARK LIBRARY
01902 556296

EP. 11|10|12

**2 4 NOV 2012**

2 2 DEC 2012

**1 1 APR 2013**

2 6 JUN 2014

- 3 SEP 2016
**1 7 MAR 2017**

2 5 SEP 2026

24 HOUR RENEWAL HOTLINE
TEL: 01902 552500

Please return/renew this item by the last date shown
Thank you for using your library

**Wolverhampton Libraries**

D0522200

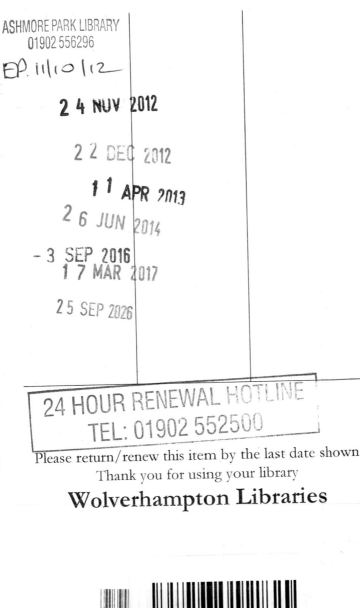

**"What would you call a one-way ticket to New York in the same envelope as a petition for divorce?"**

"Expedient."

She cursed, and her hand flew to cover her mouth.

She *never* used language like that, and honestly she hadn't even called him that in her own mind. But hearing him downplay the most painful day of her life to mere expedience was more than she could handle.

He didn't take offense. In fact he laughed. "You wouldn't be the first to think so."

Ariston in business mode was dangerous enough, but when he reverted to charming and approachable...? Perfectly fatal to her heart.

"Let me get this straight," she said, needing to get the topic of their conversation back on track. "You'll refrain from selling your shares in Dioletis Industries and provide the infusion of capital necessary, as well as the savvy business direction to keep it solvent, if I play the part of your mistress for the next three years?"

**Lucy Monroe** started reading at the age of four. After she had gone through the children's books at home, her mother caught her reading adult novels pilfered from the higher shelves on the bookcase… Alas, it was nine years before she got her hands on a Mills & Boon® Romance her older sister had brought home. She loves to create the strong alpha males and independent women who people Mills & Boon® books. When she's not immersed in a romance novel (whether reading or writing it), she enjoys travel with her family, having tea with the neighbours, gardening, and visits from her numerous nieces and nephews.

Lucy loves to hear from her readers: e-mail LucyMonroe@LucyMonroe.com, or visit www.LucyMonroe.com

**Recent titles by the same author:**

HEART OF A DESERT WARRIOR
FOR DUTY'S SAKE
THE GREEK'S PREGNANT LOVER
THE SHY BRIDE

**Did you know these are also available as eBooks?**
**Visit www.millsandboon.co.uk**

# NOT JUST THE GREEK'S WIFE

BY
LUCY MONROE

All the characters in this book have no existence outside the imagination of the author, and have no relation whatsoever to anyone bearing the same name or names. They are not even distantly inspired by any individual known or unknown to the author, and all the incidents are pure invention.

All Rights Reserved including the right of reproduction in whole or in part in any form. This edition is published by arrangement with Harlequin Enterprises II BV/S.à.r.l. The text of this publication or any part thereof may not be reproduced or transmitted in any form or by any means, electronic or mechanical, including photocopying, recording, storage in an information retrieval system, or otherwise, without the written permission of the publisher.

® and TM are trademarks owned and used by the trademark owner and/or its licensee. Trademarks marked with ® are registered with the United Kingdom Patent Office and/or the Office for Harmonisation in the Internal Market and in other countries.

First published in Great Britain 2012
by Mills & Boon, an imprint of Harlequin (UK) Limited.
Harlequin (UK) Limited, Eton House, 18-24 Paradise Road,
Richmond, Surrey TW9 1SR

© Lucy Monroe 2012

ISBN: 978 0 263 22802 1

Harlequin (UK) policy is to use papers that are natural, renewable and recyclable products and made from wood grown in sustainable forests. The logging and manufacturing process conform to the legal environmental regulations of the country of origin.

Printed and bound in Great Britain
by CPI Antony Rowe, Chippenham, Wiltshire

# NOT JUST THE GREEK'S WIFE

| WOLVERHAMPTON PUBLIC LIBRARIES | |
| --- | --- |
| XB000000165200 | |
| Bertrams | 26/09/2012 |
| | £13.50 |
| AP | 01586811 |

# CHAPTER ONE

EVEN in her exquisitely tailored designer suit, Chloe Spiridakou felt out of place in her ex-husband's swank office waiting area.

Like their marriage, the classic pink tweed skirt and blazer were two years past their runway date and didn't quite fit any longer. Stress and grief had taken their toll and peeled pounds she couldn't afford to lose from her already willowy figure.

She'd never had the best relationship with food, but after leaving Greece, Chloe had found it nearly impossible to force herself to eat at all. Some days had gone by when she simply hadn't.

But Rhea had stepped in, literally saving Chloe's life. And Chloe wasn't going to let her sister down now.

No matter how hard this meeting was for Chloe. No matter how ill-equipped she felt to deal with her ex-husband again.

It didn't help that she felt awkward and unattractive. Rail-thin, she'd also hardly slept since making this appointment and had dark circles under her eyes to prove it.

Not that Ariston was likely to notice how she looked. The fact that he was seeing her at all was still hard to fathom. Chloe had the distinct feeling that somehow her sister had got it wrong. Ariston had made no move to contact her since the day she'd walked out on their marriage—not even to ask why she'd done it.

Rather par for the course in a relationship that was by turns scorchingly passionate and emotionally distant.

Her husband had been attentive in his own way, even borderline kind at times and definitely an amazing lover, but Ariston had kept his feelings to himself. Period.

Chloe had this awful feeling that his secretary, Jean, had made the appointment and somehow forgotten to mention to Ariston who it was with.

Chloe was not looking forward to getting kicked out of his high-rise corner office once he realized it either. The urge to flee strong, she rubbed her damp palms down the pink tweed.

After everything, she'd been absolutely certain she wouldn't ever see him again, no matter how she might wish otherwise in the deepest recesses of her heart.

Yet, here she was. Waiting in his anteroom and feeling very much as if she'd like to throw up.

Or run.

Neither was an option.

"Ms. Spiridakou…"

Chloe was already standing from the first sound of Jean's voice. She swallowed convulsively. "Yes?"

"Mr. Spiridakou will see you now." Jean smiled, the expression one she reserved for the "real" people in Ariston's life.

Not feeling all that "real," Chloe returned the smile—her own effort not nearly so natural. "Thank you."

It was only a matter of a couple dozen feet to the tall double doors that led to Ariston's inner sanctum. Yet the time it took to cross the plush office carpet felt both too long and too short for Chloe's rapidly beating heart and the thoughts whirling like a dervish in her head.

The older woman opened the door on the left and ushered Chloe inside with another warm, encouraging smile.

Chloe wanted to say thank you again, for that smile,
for the sympathy lurking in the older woman's eyes, but
couldn't make her throat work. So she simply nodded before turning to survey her ex-husband's domain.

Easier to maintain her composure if she focused on the
room and not its occupant.

Ariston's New York office was exactly as Chloe remembered it. An imposing dark mahogany desk the size of a
small dining table sat in the center. Two leather armchairs
faced it with an occasional table between them.

On the other side of the large room, two deep burgundy
leather sofas faced one another across a large hand-stitched
Turkish rug that had taken a group of four women six
months to finish, working on it daily. Chloe had bought
it for Ariston on their honeymoon and was surprised he'd
kept it, but then she shouldn't be.

He wasn't a sentimental guy and it *did* match the perfectly appointed office decor just as well today as it had
five years ago.

Near the corner wall of windows, the sofa grouping
made an unexpectedly intimidating place to hold a meeting. Ariston had once told her he used the psychology of
it to set to the tone for certain business dealings.

Chloe was marginally relieved that Ariston's cerulean-
blue gaze met her green one across his monolith of a desk
instead. That tiny bit of relief did nothing to strengthen
suddenly water-weak joints in her knees as their eyes met
for the first time in two years.

She'd missed him. A lot. The constant ache inside her
had barely diminished in its intensity in the twenty-four
months spent trying to forget him.

The psychobabblers claimed time healed all wounds,

but Chloe's felt nearly as raw and excruciating as they had the day her marriage ended. She could feel every inch of ground she'd gained sliding away as emotions she didn't want to experience, much less acknowledge, washed over her.

One dark brow quirked and he asked, "Would you like coffee, or is this a flying visit?"

She opened her mouth to answer, but closed it again without saying a word, her attention wholly caught by the man in front of her.

He hadn't changed. He should have, shouldn't he?

She had. Her five-foot-eight-inch form was scarecrow skinny now and though she still highlighted her chocolate brown hair, she wore it longer in waves that settled against her shoulders.

He'd commented more than once that he liked long hair, but she'd refused to grow it out while they were married. She wasn't sure why now. Only that then, it had made her feel more independent. As if despite the fact she was in love with her business-marriage husband, she remained true to herself.

That sense of independence had been little comfort after she'd walked away from him.

Though she hadn't had a choice. After three years of marriage, she'd discovered he'd had divorce papers drawn up. As per their initial agreement. Even so, the discovery had been a crushing blow and leaving him had taken every ounce of her stubborn resolve. But her pride had demanded she make the first and irrevocable move.

Doing so hadn't been the healing balm she'd hoped. She was only twenty-five, but pain and worry had etched tiny lines around her eyes.

However, there were no new worry *or* laugh lines on his face, no early gray hairs to mark his advent into his thirties. It remained espresso dark, almost black, kept short but with a style that screamed power and money. The only hint to his Greek heritage, the slight curl in that perfectly styled hair.

Ariston was still just as devastatingly gorgeous as he'd ever been, his expression equally impossible to read and his manners impeccable.

Unexpected emotions slammed through her. Want and love and need and pain, all of it so strong, she had to force herself to keep breathing.

She hadn't left because she wanted to. She'd gone because she *had* to.

It had been two years, but shockingly, she craved him as strongly as if she'd walked out the door of the apartment in Athens yesterday.

Even sitting and wearing an impeccably tailored suit, it was clear his six-foot-three-inch frame sported the same well-honed muscles that she had enjoyed exploring so very much in their marriage bed. Not only a virgin, but wholly innocent on her wedding night, Chloe had known passion with only one man. This one.

An angel…a devil…a man capable of stirring things in her she could not afford to feel.

That dark brow rose again, his mouth tilting just the tiniest in sardonic amusement and she realized she still hadn't answered.

"No, I…I mean, yes, coffee would be lovely."

He gave the instruction to Jean and then focused that all-consuming gaze back on Chloe. "Perhaps you would care to take a seat?"

It was only then that she realized she'd frozen only a step over the threshold. Heat suffused her cheeks. "Oh, yes, of course."

She managed to make it into one of the armchairs without incident and didn't even bother stifling her sigh of relief as she did so. She'd always been rotten at games like poker. Everything she felt played across her face.

*Why had Rhea thought this was a good idea again?* Oh, yes, because Ariston had insisted. And what Ariston Spiridakou wanted, the Greek business mogul got.

Two years ago he hadn't wanted Chloe. For some inexplicable reason, now he did. Or at least to meet with her.

"To what do I owe the honor of this visit?" Ariston asked when the silence between them had stretched long enough for Jean to have come and gone, leaving aromatic coffee in her wake.

"Are you playing the cat to my mouse?" she asked with no attempt to hide her censure. "You told Rhea you wouldn't meet with her."

"Yes, but the purpose of that meeting has yet to be broached."

Oh, he was enjoying this. Playing corporate shark with the wife who'd had the audacity to walk out on him first.

Chloe fixated on preparing her drink so she didn't have to look at Ariston. If she did, she might very well give in to her sudden urge to toss her coffee cup right at his head. "Do you really need to ask?"

"It appears I do."

"Right." She took a fortifying sip of coffee. It was her favorite Sumatran blend with the hint of vanilla and cinnamon.

Jean had remembered, bless her.

Unwilling to appear the coward or play his little games, Chloe forced her eyes to meet those of her ex-husband. "I'm sure you know exactly why I'm here, but maybe you're wondering why I thought coming would be of any use? To be honest, I was pretty sure it wouldn't be, but I had to try."

There. He could put that in his pipe and smoke it. If he smoked. Which he didn't. Darn it, her mind was running away with her again.

She consciously reined in her wayward thoughts.

"For your father's sake." Ariston's tone was flat, his mouth drawn in a line that could have been disapproval, or just as easily apathy. "You would do anything for your father."

A sound of dark humor spilled from Chloe's lips before she could even think of stifling it.

*Seriously?* Had Ariston gotten to know her at all during the brief three years of their marriage? She had never once tried to pretend a closeness with her father that did not exist. That had *never* existed.

She wasn't the business-minded protégée Rhea was, garnering their father's attention in a way Chloe could never compete with. Chloe had always been the artsy one, like their mother whose paintings had hung on the walls of their home years after death had taken her from their lives.

"I haven't seen or spoken to my father in almost two years." More vehement than she intended, Chloe took a deep breath and let her gaze shift to the original El Greco hanging on the wall behind his desk in its gilt-edged frame.

She had always loved it, but the old masterpiece held no solace for her today.

Her father had sold her into marriage with no care for her feelings. When they'd been ripped asunder, rational or not, she'd laid a good portion of the blame at his door.

She might have been able to forgive him for setting her up for such heartache, but not what came after.

"I find that hard to believe."

"Really?" She shook her head, finding it difficult to believe even now that Ariston was so ignorant of her feelings, and let their gazes meet again.

His was assessing.

Was it possible that despite the fact she'd never tried to hide it, Ariston simply hadn't noticed how little interaction she had with her father? The two men had a closer relationship than she'd ever shared with the man who'd fathered her.

She was convinced Ariston knew the other businessman better than she ever would.

"Eber Dioletis only ever deigned to notice my existence when he needed a daughter to fulfill the business contract he thought would save his crumbling empire." He hadn't even sounded sorry when he'd informed her over the phone of her then-husband's actions in having divorce papers drawn up, but then Eber had had his own plans, hadn't he? "Do you know what he said when I called to tell him I was returning to New York?"

Chloe snapped her mouth shut. She hadn't meant to ask that, had had no intention of ever sharing that final humiliation with anyone. She'd never even told Rhea.

"What?" Ariston asked, his attention sharpening as if he realized she'd let something slip she didn't want to.

Hurting and lost after making the only decision she could once she'd found out about Ariston's plans to divorce her, Chloe had called her father and told him she was on her way home. She'd intended to return to the house she'd grown up in, familiar if not a warm haven of memories.

That hadn't happened.

Because her father had been and would always be a coldhearted man.

"It doesn't matter."

"I must disagree. You brought it up."

She had.

And unlike her parent, or even Ariston, Chloe was no

master prevaricator. "He had another prospect in mind for once the divorce was final."

Another arranged marriage waiting in the wings, an older businessman worth tens of millions, if not a few billion like her ex-husband. Eber had known the marriage wasn't going to last beyond its three-year term and had sought to take advantage of that fact.

To this day, she didn't know how her father had found out about the divorce papers Ariston had drawn up in New York before that final trip to Greece. She only knew that he'd had proof. The morning Ariston had flown to Hong Kong for what was supposed to be a short business trip, Eber had sent Chloe a fax—divorce papers signed by her husband and dated not two weeks before their arrival in Athens.

Though they hadn't yet been filed, much less served, there was only one interpretation of her husband's actions and once Chloe had made it, her own decisions at the end of her marriage rose up to torment her with just how naively hopeful she'd been.

"This upset you?" Ariston didn't look or sound in the least surprised by news of Eber's backup plan.

Chloe had to wonder if he'd known about it. Those two were peas in a pod, knowing things they shouldn't when it came to one of their business ventures. And hadn't her marriage to Ariston been nothing but that?

She'd tried to convince herself otherwise toward the end, but ultimately she'd been proven spectacularly wrong.

"Yes," she bit out, unable to believe even Ariston could have thought otherwise.

But then, he'd never known her as she knew him. He hadn't made the effort to do so because he'd never loved her as she loved him.

Needing some distance, even if it was contrived, she

dipped her head and took a sip of her coffee. "My father said his business associate was looking for the right trophy wife. It wouldn't even matter that I hadn't managed to get pregnant during my three years of marriage to you, since he already had three full-grown children."

"He believed you incapable of conception?" Ariston asked carefully.

"Yes." She hadn't told anyone, even her sister, about using birth control, though Rhea had been the one to suggest it in the beginning.

Rhea had believed the idea of becoming a mother immediately was why Chloe had balked at the idea of being married in a business deal. Her sister had spoken to her privately about taking measures to give herself some time before taking on the responsibility of children.

Eber would have been furious if he'd known—either about the conversation, or that Chloe had ultimately decided to act on her sister's advice. For her own best interests, something her father cared nothing about.

"And his plans for you to marry again came as an unwelcome surprise to you?" Ariston asked as if checking his facts.

"I already told you that."

Ariston's expression turned thoughtful. "He was disappointed by the results of our deal and was making the best of it."

"I'm not surprised you would see it that way. You probably would have agreed with him about the divorce settlement."

But she hadn't and in this one instance, her will had prevailed.

"I'm sorry?"

"He thought I should sign the check over to him. He said it was the least I could do for the company after you ended up with a big chunk of stock and he didn't get a billionaire son-in-law out of the deal anymore." Her voice bled not only some bitterness, but pain and she made a concentrated effort to pull her emotions back in check as she sipped her coffee.

Ariston made a sound as if she'd finally shocked him. "You didn't sign the check over, though. If you had, you couldn't have financed your new life on the West Coast."

"No. During that phone conversation, I accepted that my father sees me as nothing more than an asset to exploit," she admitted. "And I was done being treated like a bargaining chip. I wanted nothing to do with him or his company ever again."

Chloe had hung up on her father and that conversation was the last time they'd spoken.

For as much as Eber's indifference during her childhood had hurt, that knowledge hurt even more, adding more pain than she could handle to her already devastated soul.

Chloe had just lost the love of her life, even if it had ultimately been her decision, and her father's only concern had been adding to the financial coffers of Dioletis Industries. Again.

She hadn't been surprised at all to discover that Eber now expected Rhea to sacrifice her happiness to the altar of Dioletis Industries. Chloe was here to make sure that didn't happen.

Her own marriage had been a bust, but Rhea's could be saved. If her sister could get out from under the burden of a failing empire and their father's expectations.

It wasn't just Rhea who had asked Chloe for help either. Rhea's husband, Samuel, had come to Chloe, desperate to save his marriage but equally certain there was only one chance to do it. A chance he wasn't sure Rhea would take even if it was offered.

Samuel wanted his wife back from the grasping jaws of Dioletis Industries. He wanted a family, something Rhea had said she wanted as well...before she'd been forced to take over chairmanship of the company.

Now Rhea was too busy trying to run a failing company to see the cost to her personal life and Chloe knew that without intervention, her beloved sister could turn out way too much like their father. And not even realize it.

"You never expressed discontent with your lot while we were married...at least not verbally." Ariston interrupted her thoughts in a precise New York drawl that showed none of his Greek heritage.

Her gaze flew back up to his. "Why would I have told you how I felt about being used as a bargaining chip in a business deal?"

It wasn't his problem and the truth was, she'd been almost certain it wouldn't matter to him.

Besides, in the beginning, she'd considered they were in a similar boat—her father pushing her into marriage for the sake of the company, Ariston's grandfather pushing for him to settle down with a nice Greek girl.

More American than Greek in many ways, Ariston had insisted on a woman raised in his adopted home country.

Chloe had met both men's requirements, her Greek heritage and family winning approval from the older Spiridakou and her American citizenship garnering Ariston's acceptance. The fact that marriage to her would get him significant shares in what had looked like a thriving private concern at the time hadn't hurt anything either.

"Perhaps you owed it to me, since I was the other side of that bargain and it resulted in our marriage."

"A marriage you would have cheerfully jettisoned? Give me a break. We didn't share confidences and you certainly weren't interested in my heart." Whatever she was doing

here, they weren't going to rewrite history to his speci-
fications.

"I'm not the one who walked out."

"You had divorce papers drawn up and ready to serve.
No doubt they attempted to do so while you were in Hong
Kong, but I'd already left for New York." At least she'd as-
sumed that had been his plan.

She hadn't even bothered having her own papers cre-
ated, knowing his were sufficient to the task. The speed
with which she'd been served upon returning to the States
had certainly implied she'd been right.

"What are you talking about?" Ariston asked in a tone
that could have frozen rolling lava.

"Stop it," she demanded. "I'm not playing these games
with you."

"Explain yourself."

"You. Had. Divorce. Papers. Drawn. Up," she enunci-
ated very slowly and clearly. "Before we ever left New
York for our spring trip to Athens."

Following Ariston's lifelong practice since reaching
adulthood, he and Chloe had lived one month in four in
Greece. It made for a lot of travel, but she hadn't minded.

And multinational tycoon that he was, that sort of thing
was simply everyday living for Ariston.

"How did you know that?" he asked with unperturbed
curiosity, making no effort to deny it at least.

"My father faxed me a copy."

"And he got them how?"

"I have no idea. Probably through the same under-
handed channels you use."

"I do not engage in corporate espionage." Ariston
sounded genuinely offended.

She was hard-pressed not to give in to a gallows-style
humor. "Call it what you like."

"Highly developed business acumen and contacts."

"Fine."

"So you left because you believed I was going to file for divorce?" he asked with a very odd inflection to his tone.

She wanted to scream, *Yes, that's right,* but she simply shrugged. "I left because that was the only course open to me at that point. Our marriage wasn't working."

"I thought it was working very well."

"You would." And still he'd had the papers drawn up, presumably because in the one important area, to him at least, their marriage had been a bust.

She hadn't gotten pregnant.

"What is that supposed to mean?"

She shook her head, not about to admit her love for him and how the emotional distance between them had killed her a little more each day. "We wanted different things."

"On that I would have to agree." Again the strange tone, but this time it was tinged with an inexplicable anger.

Right. Their marriage hadn't been what either of them had wanted. She'd known that. Hearing him say it shouldn't hurt now. It did. But it shouldn't.

One thing was certain—*she* needed to move forward with her life. Irrevocably.

She'd thought she'd done that—leaving him, accepting the divorce without contest. Moving across country and opening her shop and gallery had been her way of cementing the break.

But if she couldn't get a handle on the memories and emotions that had hurt far more than they'd ever helped, she was never going to be free of him, Chloe realized with awful clarity.

# CHAPTER TWO

ARISTON sipped from his cup—matching china to hers that probably cost more than most of the paintings she had for sale in her gallery—and made a face. "I never understood your taste for flavored coffee."

"Surely Jean could have made you the dark Arabic blend you prefer." Chloe had always thought his beverage of preference tasted like espresso even when it was prepared in the automatic drip.

And to her way of thinking, espresso belonged in gourmet coffees with lots of milk and yummy flavorings. The thought of drinking it straight out of one of those tiny cups always made her shudder.

He dismissed her suggestion with a wave of his hand. "That would have required preparing two pots, not one."

Chloe sincerely doubted it. If Jean didn't have one of those fancy single-cup coffeemakers in the small kitchen behind her own office, Chloe would be shocked.

Which meant that Jean had served Ariston Chloe's favorite on purpose. Why?

"You told her ahead of time to make my favorite," Chloe guessed, gobsmacked at the idea and wholly unable to understand what he hoped to gain by doing so.

She was the first to admit she didn't begin to operate on the Machiavellian level he did when it came to business, but this was beyond her. It was as if he was trying to be accommodating and when it came to business, she knew her ex-husband was anything but.

Maybe he was trying to lull her into a false sense of complacency? To what purpose? He held all the cards in the deck, not just the good ones, and they both knew it.

"Naturally. It was only polite."

"If you say so." Realizing how rude that sounded, which had not been her intention, she added, "Thank you."

"That aside," he said as if the coffee discussion had derailed them from talking about what really mattered. "Entering such an arrangement with unexpressed resentments for its terms wasn't very ethical of you, was it?" he chided.

*Ethical?* Was the man serious?

Needing to move, she jumped up and walked over to the nearest wall of windows. She stared down at the city, people and cars made tiny by distance. "Do you honestly believe I didn't express my unhappiness at the idea of quitting art school and being forced into what amounted to a medieval marriage bargain to my father?"

Before she'd met Ariston and realized that dreams could change.

"Eber implied to my grandfather that you were entirely on board with the plan." Ariston spoke from behind her.

She wasn't surprised that in her agitation, she hadn't realized he'd moved.

She didn't bother to turn and face him, however. "Right. And you both believed him. It never occurred to you that he might have simply cut funding to my schooling and living expenses, effectively getting me evicted from my dorm?"

Instead of the city below, she saw the face of the dean of her college when the older man had been forced to give

Chloe the news. They'd been midway through the term and she'd been sure her father couldn't demand his money back.

But apparently powerful men could do things other mere mortals couldn't.

"I suppose you never guessed he might freeze my accounts because they were all in his name, too? No, I doubt you even thought about why I agreed to that barbaric bargain."

"Bargains such as ours are common enough among the world's powerful in both business and politics. You needn't act as if you were sold into marriage in some medieval contract in which you had no say or personal rights."

She spun to face him, old anger brought about by a feeling of utter helplessness rising to the fore. "Wasn't I? I was a twenty-year-old college student, Ariston! I'd only ever worked part-time in an art supply store for hobby money. I had no clue how to even begin going about getting my life back when he took it away."

Ariston's handsome face set in unreadable lines, but emotion she couldn't name flickered briefly in his blue eyes. "You never told me any of this."

"By the time I met you, both my father and my sister had put the emotional screws in." And Chloe had forgiven Rhea, though she doubted she ever would her father. Rhea's motives hadn't all been about the company; she'd believed the marriage would be good for Chloe, too.

Chloe laughed harshly. "Rhea made it clear that if she weren't already married, she would have willingly sacrificed herself for the good of our family and our heritage. That's how she and my father see the company, as if it is a living entity deserving of every manner of sacrifice and effort."

She didn't blame her sister. Not even a little. They'd both

been raised in the same emotional wasteland and each of them had found different ways to cope.

Rhea had sought their father's love and approval the only way she'd known how—through the business. The one and only thing he ever had truly loved.

"I am aware."

"Then I met you." And against all odds and what her mind told her was possible, Chloe had fallen for her Greek tycoon on first sight. Fully, irrevocably and completely.

His hands fisted at his side as if he wanted to reach out, but he forced himself not to. "And expressed none of your concerns."

"No. You and my father had made your plans, but I had hopes that complying with them might lead to something else." Foolish, youthful hopes that she now knew for the ridiculous fantasies they were.

She dropped her head, not wanting to see his face. Not being able to bear it right then.

"Look at me," he commanded, as if he'd read her mind and was truly bothered by her thoughts.

She considered denying him, but what was the point? This conversation had to happen so they could have the one she'd come for. Rhea's happiness depended on it.

And Rhea deserved to be happy. In her own way, she'd sacrificed more than Chloe ever had because she'd never walked away.

Chloe lifted her head, and whatever Ariston saw in her face made his crease in a frown. "What hopes?"

"They don't matter anymore." They never had, not to him…not to her father.

"I would still prefer to know what they were."

"No," she said with absolute implacability. She'd shared all the confidences she was going to with this man.

His look assessed her. "You have changed."

"Yes."

He stepped closer. "In every way, I wonder?"

Shock paralyzed her as his nearness brought a wholly unexpected reaction. She'd thought her libido had died with her marriage, but her body was telling her just how wrong she'd been.

*She wanted him.*

She managed to move back, but somehow she gained no distance between them as he matched her step for step until she stood against the window. His scent and the heat of his body surrounded her, bringing back memories that haunted her dreams, that made her body ache with a longing she'd thought gone forever.

Long masculine fingers curved around her nape, his thumb brushing the sensitive flesh behind her ear. "There was a time when this drove you crazy. Does it still, I wonder?"

She shook her head, but not to deny it, simply to try to clear her mind enough to speak. To tell him to let her go, to move back. For heaven's sake.

Only the words didn't come. Couldn't come.

Because no matter what her mind screamed she should say, she desperately wanted to beg him to do more, move closer, touch her…give her what she'd once had the right to every night.

Ariston's head lowered. "I wonder," he said again. "Will your lips taste as sweet as they did two years ago?"

She had no answer for him, but a reciprocating question spun round and round in her mind as his lips covered hers. Would he taste as good? Would he taste like love, even if he didn't love her—like he'd used to?

Would this kiss hurt or heal?

Would it make it harder or easier for her to continue in

her quest to move on? Cutting herself off from him without any sort of closure certainly hadn't worked.

Only risking it would give the answer to that one, and something Chloe had never been was a coward. She let the kiss come.

It was not tentative, but sought to determine her susceptibility. She wondered what he found even as her mind warred with her heart over the wisdom of letting this melding of lips continue. He kissed her as if he had every right to do so, as if they were still married.

As if she was his.

It was strange and horribly wonderful and wholly unexpected.

And she let him, trying to determine if in that moment he still felt as if he was hers, and coming to the abrupt and almost awful revelation that he did.

His lips moved over hers, his tongue gliding along the seam of her mouth, gently demanding entrance.

Chloe's mind screamed for her to protest this assault on her senses. It was too dangerous, she realized perhaps too late.

Finally her mouth opened to do it, but that only gave him the opportunity he wanted.

And maybe, just maybe, that's exactly what she'd intended after all.

His tongue plundered, his lips moving against hers, and drew forth a response only this man had ever engendered. Desire like liquid fire pooled deep inside her and she moaned against his lips. He made a harsh sound of approval, deepening the kiss—if that was possible.

The one outcome to this meeting she'd never expected would be that Ariston would kiss her, or that his nearness and touch would reawaken the sexual hunger within her.

It was too much and not enough.

His free hand pressed against her back, so their bodies came into full, glorious contact. It electrified her.

And made her see a truth she'd hidden from.

For two years she'd craved this very thing, but with a gut-wrenching certainty that it would never again be hers. So she'd suppressed her desires to hold the pain of unrequited need at bay.

Now he was offering to assuage that need and her body was letting her know she'd gone too long without. After three years of a marriage that had included a steady diet of truly mind-blowing sex, she'd cut herself off completely.

And her carefully suppressed libido wasn't happy.

Not even a little bit.

She was no slave to her body's desires, or at least she didn't think she was, but the reasons for not letting him do this were disappearing in the mist of lust boiling through her.

And in a moment of clarity she realized she wasn't going to give this moment up. Not for the sake of propriety, or what it might cost her, or anything else. No matter how temporary, whatever came later, or however long this physical connection lasted, she was giving herself up to it for now.

She deserved it.

She might even need it, this chance to say goodbye that she hadn't given herself the first time around.

She already knew the pain of loss and she was strong enough to withstand it again, but she deserved some pleasure for all her pain.

She wasn't worried that this would make it harder to get over him, or undo the strides she'd made forward in doing so. Because one thing that had become painfully obvious from the moment she walked into his office and looked him in the eye for the first time since leaving Greece, she was not over this man and there were no strides forward.

There was just learning to live without. Which she had done and could do again, *but not right now.*

The aftermath would come soon enough.

For once, she was going to take something for herself before worrying about the interests of others. She could still ask Ariston what Rhea needed her to. And he would most likely say no, just as he would have before this amazing kiss, but that was for later.

Right now was for them, well, for her...but he certainly seemed every bit as into it as she was.

With that thought, Chloe let her body relax into his, feeling the evidence of his arousal pressing against her stomach. Oh, yes, he was most definitely enjoying himself, too.

He made a sound of triumph and lifted her, carrying her to the couch without ever once breaking the all-consuming kiss. He laid her down, but pulled away.

"No." She reached for him; she knew he wanted it, too.

His eyes burned with a passion she'd become very familiar with during their short marriage. "I must lock the door. It would not do to shock Jean's sensibilities."

It was so like something he'd said once before when they'd made love...had sex...in this very office during their marriage. Chloe was overwhelmed by a sense of déjà vu and couldn't respond.

He didn't wait for her to anyway, but moved quickly to the door. The sound of the lock clicking into place was loud in the cavernous office, silent but for their excited breaths.

He had already removed his tie and was working on his shirt buttons by the time he came back to her and Chloe's breath stalled only to start again with a quick pant. "I'd forgotten how efficient you can be."

"Did you really?" he asked, sounding like he didn't believe it at all.

"Maybe not." Honesty compelled her to admit, "You're not very forgettable."

"Nor, *yineka mou,* are you."

He'd used to call her that all the time. It could mean "my woman," or "my wife," depending on the intent. Neither fit any longer, but she wasn't going to argue about him getting possessive during sex.

She liked it too much. Besides, he'd told her she was hard to forget, too.

She didn't mind hearing that at all.

He finished undressing without an ounce of false modesty, his eyes caressing her with a heated stare the whole time. He didn't suggest she do likewise and she wasn't surprised, or worried.

Apparently he still liked the idea of undressing her as much as he used to.

So she lay there, getting her own Greek tycoon striptease and enjoying every second of it. Even if it was done with moves more efficient than overtly sexual, her excitement escalated to near unbearable levels.

Her body vibrated with the need to have him inside her, her nipples ached to have his lips on them, her core convulsing involuntarily as if in memory of what it felt like to be joined.

She loved him. She'd never been able to stop. But right now? She just *wanted* him.

"You look very pleased with yourself." He didn't quite smile, but he didn't seem to mind either.

She shrugged. "Pleased with what I see, more like. You keep your body in amazing shape, Ariston."

He had changed in this one way. He'd been gorgeously muscular before, but now his body was hard all over and while he didn't look like some kind of muscle bound Hulk, he clearly took his regime more seriously these days.

"I work out every day. Cardio in the morning, weights at night."

"That's pretty dedicated." He'd used to only work out once a day, five days a week.

"It helps me sleep."

"I don't remember you needing much sleep."

He didn't answer, but dropped to his knees beside her, his hand reaching to caress her under her suit jacket. "Undressing you is like unwrapping a present."

He'd used to say that too and she found herself suddenly too choked to answer. So she just smiled, the first one that came naturally to her since arriving in New York.

"Do you look the same under these layers?" he asked as his lips whispered down the side of her face to her neck.

"I'm a little thinner."

He stopped moving, lifting his head to stare at her. "Surely you had no extra weight to lose."

For the first time, trepidation filled her. She looked a bit more like a scarecrow than sexpot these days, not that she'd ever had a curvaceous figure.

He didn't give her anxiety a chance to build. Showing he read her, at least in the bedroom, every bit as well as he'd ever done, he kissed away her worries as his hands began work on her blouse.

Words whispered against her skin that she could not quite make out as he took off her clothes, his fingertips leaving a heated trail of pleasure as he touched each newly revealed patch of skin.

By the time he had her completely naked, she was shivering with need. He'd very purposefully not touched her most erogenous zones, but had still managed to bring her to the point of begging.

Only biting firmly on her bottom lip was keeping the words inside.

He lifted his head to smile at her, his expression knowing. "You never were very patient the first time out of the box."

"Since this may be our only time, maybe you should get a move on," she gritted out, though in sexual frustration, not anger.

His expression turned intent. "You think so, do you?"

"You live in New York, when you're even in the country. I live in Oregon. We're not exactly well suited for casual hookups."

"On that, at least, we agree."

She didn't get a chance to ask what he meant by that because he touched her breasts. Finally. And she nearly climaxed without him ever going near her clitoris.

But he remembered exactly what kind of touch to her nipples and breasts pleasured her the most and was intent on giving it to her. In abundance. He used his hands and mouth to bring her body taut like a bowstring and then one hand slipped between her legs.

Her mouth opened to scream and he kissed her, swallowing the sound as the ultimate pleasure crashed over her in a tsunami of bliss.

He pulled back, his fingers still touching her, but gently, causing small aftershocks to wrack her body. "It has been a while for you, I think."

She might be blissed out. She might even still love him. But no way was she answering that implied question. "None of your business."

"Your body does not lie."

"Think what you like." She looked away, knowing her expression would tell him the truth even if her mouth didn't.

Then a very disturbing thought occurred to her. Was he using sex to disturb her equilibrium further in this business game only he seemed to know the rules to?

A gentle hand brushed her cheek. "Hey, stay with me, Chloe. We are far from finished."

"No more questions about my private life."

"Only one."

She glared at him, sealing her lips.

"Are you in a relationship?"

"Surely whatever spies you have watching your business interests told you the answer to that."

"I do not have investigators watching you." By his tone, he considered he'd shown restraint and expected her to appreciate that fact.

She, on the other hand, couldn't think of a reason he would have wanted to in the first place.

Something of her thoughts must have shown on her face because he said, "There is very little related to any of my business interests that I do not know."

Okay, but again, why? She wasn't one of his business interests any longer. Even though he still held a big chunk of shares in Dioletis Industries, she had nothing to do with the company and even less to do with him.

Their currently somewhat intimate circumstances aside.

"Arrogant much?" she asked with a heavy dose of sarcasm.

She used to find his arrogance charming. Maybe part of her still did, but really—what had she been thinking?

He merely smiled.

Well, Mr. Arrogance *hadn't* known she was on birth control during their short-lived marriage. And technically, it had been just another business arrangement. So, he didn't know everything now, did he?

Despite falling head over heels for the gorgeous jerk,

the one thing she'd been adamant about was that she wasn't trapping him or herself into marriage through a child. Not unless they both wanted to be there permanently, and obviously he hadn't.

"Do you honestly think I'd be on this couch if I had someone waiting for me back in Oregon?" she asked, to get her mind back where it needed to be.

She wanted this, and even *she* wasn't going to ruin it for herself.

"No, but I would appreciate hearing the words." He almost sounded humble.

Which was enough of a shock for her to acquiesce that much. "I'm not in a relationship."

"Good."

"I assume you aren't in one either?" Not that she thought for a minute they defined the word the same way.

They certainly hadn't agreed on what it meant to be married.

"No."

"Then we can continue without guilt."

"*Ne*. We will continue." That single slip into Greek to say yes indicated more than his body coiled tightly with sexual tension, or even his hard-on, that Ariston was not in absolute control.

And then the tension snapped and the whirlwind that was her tycoon lover for the afternoon swept over her with touches and kisses and bodies rocking together until she spread her legs, silently begging him to enter her.

He grabbed a condom from the pocket of his slacks and she tried very hard not to think why he might carry those around. "Help me put it on."

She nodded, and with trembling hands, did exactly that. He groaned as her fingers rolled the condom down his generous length.

Stilling above her, he implored, "Don't move. Not your hand, not your body. Nothing. Please."

It was as out of control as she'd ever seen him and she did as he asked. His eyes shut, his head thrown back in repose, he took several deep breaths, letting each one out more slowly than the last.

When he looked down at her again, his azure eyes were dark with desire. "Now."

"Yes."

He pressed inside her and her body convulsed around him. Not in climax, but in absolute pleasure and relief at finally being connected to him in this way again. For her, it was a moment so profound, she could not speak.

He did not look as if he needed words, but seemed lost in his own passion, and for that she was grateful.

Even more so when that passion took them on another journey to fulfillment, this time her orgasm gripping her entire body in contractions so intense that though she opened her mouth to scream again, no sound came out.

He muffled his own shout of completion in the juncture of her neck and shoulder, kissing her over and over again between words like *Yes,* and *So good,* and *Fantastic.*

Afterward, they cleaned up in his office's en suite, neither speaking, but the silence between them not really awkward at all.

It should have been.

She should be having all sorts of regrets, but she wasn't. She'd wanted this and had enjoyed it far more than even she had thought possible.

She realized he wasn't feeling quite so sanguine when he looked up from buttoning his shirt, his expression clearly chagrined. "I did not intend to jump you in my office like that."

"I'm not complaining."

"Yes, well…" He seemed at a loss for words at her response.

"We're both adults, Ariston. Whatever else was between us, the sex was always good."

"Better than," he agreed firmly.

She found herself grinning, really grinning, for the first time in a very long time. "Much better than."

"Have dinner with me tonight."

Without thinking, she reached out to straighten his tie. "Okay."

They still had to talk about the company and his shares and what he planned to do with them.

"Good." He stepped back, forcing her hands to drop away. "Jean can give you restaurant and time details. We can discuss whatever it is you came here to see me about then. We seem to have used up our time with other things."

"I'll stop by her desk on the way out."

"I will see you then." He left the bathroom and was back into full business mode, even taking a call when she followed him a few moments later.

She'd needed time to collect herself.

So the silence hadn't been awkward, but she wasn't giving him five stars on postorgasmic afterglow either.

He took a sip of what had to be cold coffee by now and grimaced. A small tendril of satisfaction unfurled in her. Ariston wasn't picky about the temperature of his coffee, just the taste.

And right now he was suffering through her favorite. Whatever the reason for that, it made her feel just a little like she was getting her own back.

# CHAPTER THREE

ARISTON set the phone down, the need for pretense gone now that Chloe had left his office.

Feeling unsettled in a way that was totally alien to his nature, Ariston cursed volubly in Greek. Just like the first time around, nothing was as it seemed with Chloe.

None of the motives he'd attributed to her actions during their marriage withstood the revelations she'd made in his office. And damn it to hell, he hadn't intended to have sex with her. Not yet.

No matter how much he'd enjoyed it and knew the pleasure to be reciprocal, he didn't like being out of control. And he had been. He didn't like deviating from the plan. And he had done.

Frustration and a touch of something he absolutely refused to acknowledge, but someone else might label fear, went through him. He took a deliberate sip of his coffee and the unwelcome flavor pouring across his tongue hit him as another testament to his loss of control.

With another low curse, he threw the cup against the bulletproof glass of his oversize office windows. The sound of shattering crockery was a lot more satisfying than his own thoughts.

Jean opened the door almost immediately. "Is everything all right in here?"

"Is she gone?" Ariston demanded.

"Yes."

"You gave her instructions for where to meet for dinner?" Plans he'd made before Chloe ever set foot in his office this morning.

"I did." Jean looked at the broken china cup and coffee spilled against the window. "I know you don't like that blend, but was that entirely necessary?"

"Have maintenance in to clean it up when I've left," he instructed without answering her gentle gibe.

She nodded, her expression revealing concern he had no desire to see. "Do you need anything?"

"Just privacy." The words came out harsher than intended, but he wasn't about to apologize.

Jean, being the highly efficient and intelligent PA that she was, closed the door with a soft snick, disappearing on the other side.

His meeting with Chloe ran over and over in his mind, his superior brain having difficulty aligning newly discovered realities with beliefs he had held for two years.

She hadn't confirmed it, but he now believed there was a strong possibility that his wife had walked out on him because of the divorce papers her father had told her about.

Divorce papers Ariston had drawn up in his absolute fury at discovering Chloe's deceitful actions.

Actions that no longer fit into the scenario Ariston had first assigned to them, but behavior that was no less a heinous betrayal of both his grandfather and himself regardless of what had motivated it.

How else could he see her use of birth control when one of the major reasons for their marriage contract was to provide his grandfather with the certainty of the next generation of Spiridakous?

Ariston had believed that marrying Chloe as part of

a business bargain would take the messy emotional side out of his need for children to pass the Spiridakou empire onto. His own father had messed up spectacularly in that arena repeatedly.

And Ariston's one foray into the world of romance had had him crashing and burning, not to mention losing several million dollars on a business deal gone bad in the bargain.

So when his grandfather had come to him and asked him to consider a contractual marriage to ensure the next generation, after careful consideration, Ariston had agreed. As he'd reminded Chloe, it wasn't so uncommon among the men at his level of power and wealth.

He knew Eber Dioletis was looking for a single investor to infuse capital into his company.

Eber didn't want to give enough shares of the company for the investment capital he expected in return, but the marriage deal made it possible for both men to find a win-win.

Emotions were messy and devastating.

Business was something Ariston understood and knew how to control, so finding a wife as the result of a business deal appealed very much.

He now realized his certainty that a business marriage would come without the complications he'd sworn off, not once, but twice in his life—first because of his parents' devastating mistakes and then because of his own—was one of the reasons he'd been so livid with Chloe for lying to him.

She'd let him down personally, but more important, Chloe had betrayed him on a business level, just as Shannon had done. Only this time, Ariston's grandfather had been hurt as well and Ariston found that untenable.

The one person in his life he could trust and wanted to protect, and Chloe had betrayed them both.

Ariston hadn't discovered what she'd been up to until a couple of months before their third anniversary. He'd been looking for his wife's favorite pair of earrings so he could have a complementary necklace and bracelet made as a gift to celebrate the occasion.

He'd also hoped to use the jewelry to soften her toward having fertility tests done. Ariston hadn't said anything, but he'd been to his own doctor and tests had confirmed that there should be no problem with conception coming from his side.

He'd thought Chloe might need fertility treatments because three years of sex at least once a day, often more frequently, should have resulted in pregnancy.

For a woman not on birth control.

Ariston had never found the earrings. What he *had* found was a partially used packet of birth control pills in the upper drawer of Chloe's jewelry armoire.

No matter how she wanted to look at it, Chloe had affirmed to both Ariston and his grandfather that *she* wanted children before she ever signed the contract they'd negotiated with Eber Dioletis.

She'd tacked on an *eventually,* but Ariston had assumed the eventually would come within the initial three-year parameter of their marriage contract.

Apparently, he'd been wrong.

What was bothering him now was the possibility—no, *probability*—he'd been equally wrong about other things, as well.

Chloe had not been on board with her father's idea of marrying her off in another business contract advantageous to Dioletis Industries. Ariston had known the older man's plans in that line had fallen through, but he'd assumed it was because of actions on Ariston's part.

He'd made subtle but unmistakable promises regarding the future of the other man's business interests if he married Chloe. Ariston had followed that up by allowing his displeasure at the thought of his ex-wife married to someone else leak into the financial community.

It would take a brave or very stupid man to buck the Spiridakou empire.

No one had. Or so he thought.

It had never occurred to Ariston that Chloe might have refused any other marriage deal outright, that those threats might be unnecessary.

However, that made a lot more sense of the fact that she'd made a new life for herself across country. Her claim she'd had nothing to do with her father or Dioletis Industries in two years rang true and was too easily checked. As she had to know it would be.

He'd told Chloe he hadn't had her watched by a private investigator, and he hadn't, but now he regretted that choice.

He'd been too focused on Eber and Dioletis Industries and maneuvering her father into an untenable situation for which there was only one out—giving Ariston what he wanted. He hadn't been focused enough on the woman who had been his wife.

Most telling, for Ariston at any rate, was that he had no trouble adjusting his view of her to something other than a mercenary witch, willing to defraud a trusting old man to get what she wanted for her father's company, that he'd believed her to be for the past two years.

His instincts had told him Chloe was an innocent, but he'd allowed his knowledge of her deceit to override them.

His new view cast his full-on revenge plans in a different light and opened the door to other possibilities he hadn't considered.

He hadn't gotten where he was by ignoring potential avenues and opportunities either. In fact, he was known for his ability to change his train of thought to a new track with lightning speed and efficiency.

Their discussion earlier today would imply that whatever Chloe's reasons for using the pill, unswerving loyalty to her father and his company was not one of them.

He had no choice but to acknowledge that it appeared she'd been far more her father's pawn than the black queen on Eber's side of the chessboard as Ariston had once believed.

Well before their last trip to Greece, Ariston had known Eber was courting other businessmen for another monetarily motivated wedding for his daughter.

At first, he'd assumed the rumors were about his oldest, Rhea, whose marriage Eber had never approved of. The marriage was the only thing Rhea had ever bucked her father's will regarding and Ariston wouldn't have put it past the other man to force his daughter into a divorce.

Only later, after discovering the birth control, had Ariston taken Eber's rumored overtures as irrefutable proof of Chloe's duplicity. He'd believed that she planned to walk away from their marriage as soon as the contract was completed.

It had surprised him that the family would give up stock in the still privately held company so easily. According to the terms of the contract, Ariston controlled the shares placed in a trust for the first three years of their marriage. If, after three years, either he or Chloe filed for divorce, he kept the rather large chunk of stock.

Well worth the fifty-million-dollar investment.

If Ariston had divorced Chloe before the three-year

term, though, he would have forfeited the stock, and vice versa if Chloe had filed for legal separation or divorce during that time.

However, if a child resulted from their marriage, said child would then own the shares, which Ariston would only be trustee of until the child's twenty-first year.

In addition, the terms of any divorce settlement would change significantly in Chloe's favor once a child had been conceived. She had every monetary reason in the world to get pregnant and Ariston had wanted it that way, assuming the incentives would be enough to dictate the direction of their relationship.

He'd been wrong and he did not enjoy that state of events. At all.

Regardless, whatever it *had* been, he now very much doubted that Chloe's use of birth control had been part of a plot to bilk him and his grandfather of fifty million dollars.

Because he still owned the stock as per the agreement and even if they didn't realize it, the precarious state of Dioletis Industries did not rest on Eber's shoulders. No matter how archaic some of his business practices.

As ignorant of the birth control as Ariston, Eber must have assumed Ariston would be the one to end the marriage at the three-year mark because Chloe had not conceived. Hence his investigations into Ariston's legal actions.

Make no mistake, Ariston had every intention of finding out how the other man had gotten hold of the papers, but he understood the attempts to do so now.

A small spark of satisfaction flared at the knowledge Eber had been no more aware of his daughter's efforts to prevent pregnancy than Ariston had been.

* * *

Ariston arrived at the restaurant right on time for the eight-o'clock reservation, but Chloe had already been seated.

Her now shoulder-length brown hair with its golden highlights was an unmistakable beacon at his favorite table. She appeared to be enjoying a jumbo shrimp cocktail. A mutual favorite of theirs.

"I am not late, I hope," he said as he took the chair across from her.

She looked up, a wry twist to her lips. "You know you aren't. But since you divorced me, I've been living more like a normal person and I usually eat dinner around six. I was starving, to tell you the truth."

He was pleased to see her eating at all and thought her claims she *normally* ate somewhat of an exaggeration.

She had lost weight since the divorce and he would prefer to see her put it back on. For her health's sake. Not because her overthin figure had turned him off. He wasn't sure anything could.

For whatever reason, his libido was turned to her signal to near devastating effect.

But she'd never had much spare weight to begin with, having an indifferent attitude toward food that he had wondered about at times during their marriage.

The slightest cold or flu had her off her feet and losing pounds she couldn't afford off her willowy five-foot-eight-inch figure.

He should inquire as to whether she'd been ill recently. That would account for her more gaunt appearance now.

For the present, he simply said mildly, "Well, that looks good. I hope you ordered me one as well."

Her green eyes twinkled as she nodded at the waiter, hovering nearby. "Oh, I thought you could do without."

The waiter arrived with Ariston's matching appetizer. They took a moment to order their entrées.

"You like to tease the bear." Ariston gave her a mock frown. "I had forgotten that."

"Really? I thought you said I was memorable." Something shifted in her expression, but then she was smiling again, if with less sparkle than he remembered. "But you meant *sexually,* didn't you?"

He was too smart to agree with her. He might have played the fool during their marriage, but he wasn't one. Not really.

"There are many things I remember about you, Chloe." That, at least, was the truth.

Her green gaze narrowed speculatively. "I imagine I was the first woman to ever leave you. That would have made me memorable, I suppose."

"That's the thing about imagination. It's not real."

Her shock was palpable. "I didn't know you'd had any serious relationships. I can't believe she ditched you either."

"Why not? You did."

"I didn't have a choice."

"Because we wanted different things," he mocked. "Perhaps my memory is faulty, but it was you in those discussions with me and my grandfather via video conference saying you wanted children eventually and that you agreed to the marriage."

"I'm not the one who filed for divorce."

"I wouldn't have been either, if you'd still been there when I got back from Hong Kong."

Both her expression and the sound that came out of her mouth said she didn't believe him.

"Shannon was my one and only serious girlfriend," he said, rather than trying to convince Chloe of something Ariston would rather forget himself.

"When?"

"A long time ago. I was younger than you were when we married."

Interest burned bright in Chloe's emerald gaze. "How young?"

"Nineteen."

"How old was she?" Chloe asked, proving an insight he didn't expect.

"Twenty-seven." And Shannon had had an entire universe worth more experience than he had with sex and the male-female thing.

He'd avoided it because of what he'd seen in his parents' marriages, so he'd been entirely unprepared for a piranha like Shannon to come into his life.

Chloe stopped eating, fiddling with her silverware instead. "How long did it last?"

"Long enough for her to gather enough inside information so her father could steal a multimillion-dollar deal out from under me." Long enough for him to tell Shannon that he loved her and wanted to be together always.

Even then, he'd been jaded about marriage, so when she'd broached the subject, he'd said they didn't need legal bindings to know what they were to each other. It had been all romance at the time, only later had he given thanks for that one small foresight.

"I…oh…" Chloe frowned, her eyes troubled. "It wasn't like that with us."

"Wasn't it?"

"No, of course not. I didn't try to get any deals for my father."

"You got him a lot of cash."

"That was your idea…yours and his. I wasn't even brought in until the deal between you two was negotiated."

"True." He frowned, annoyed by the fact that their discussion had already gone off script to what he'd planned.

"We got sidetracked rather spectacularly earlier. You never answered my question."

For several seconds Chloe looked confused, but then her expression cleared, only to turn into a frown. "You mean why I'd asked to meet with you? Are you still pretending not to know?"

"It is no pretense. You have agreed that you've changed, implied there is no love lost between you and your father, and yet here you are."

"Because my sister asked me to fall at your feet in supplication. And because her husband begged me to save my sister." Chloe shrugged her thin shoulders. "I don't think I have that power, but I'll try."

The image her words evoked made his slacks uncomfortably tight, but he merely said, "For the sake of your family's fortune."

Now was not the time to be sidetracked by sexual innuendo or fantasizing.

"For the sake of my *family,* or at least the ones that still matter to me," Chloe said with conviction. "But Rhea also reminded me of the hundreds of people employed by Dioletis Industries. I can't turn my back on all those families without at least asking you to show a little mercy."

Her expression indicated she had little hope in the success of her request, but that it was important enough to her to try. That was easy to believe. Even in their first meeting, Chloe had evinced concern for the employees of her father's company. No doubt their welfare had been one of the screws her father had turned five years ago.

And Rhea was using it again now, to great effect.

Ariston was tempted to shake his ex-wife and demand if she didn't realize she was being used again. However, he had his own plans and they didn't include pointing out weaknesses he wanted to exploit as well.

"This is about the rumors circulating that I plan to offload my stock in Dioletis Industries."

The privately held company had gone public the year before in a bid to save it. It might have worked if Ariston hadn't been working behind the scenes, but as it stood the company wavered precariously on the precipice of bankruptcy. It would take only a simple shove on the right leverage point to push it over, and Ariston held that leverage.

In more ways than one, the most obvious being his chunk of stock that if he unloaded onto the market in one big block would devalue the rest until the company's viability would be placed in question. At that point, its creditors would have no choice other than to demand bankruptcy proceedings.

Particularly those under Ariston's financial umbrella. The Spiridakou name was no longer on all of the company's concerns and that worked well for Ariston in times like these.

"Partly." She sighed and looked away, a telling response.

Ah, so, as he'd expected and hoped, the Dioletis family wanted more from him than his promise to hold on to his stock.

Finally the script was going according to plan. "Mercy has no place in business. Surely your father taught you that."

"I don't share my father's views and particularly not in that regard." Chloe glared at him, clearly offended.

He almost smiled. This was turning out to be almost too easy. "If I don't sell my shares, the company as it stands will only stay afloat another year, maybe two at the most."

"Samuel mentioned that and Rhea confirmed it."

At least Rhea had been forthright with Chloe. Perhaps the sister wasn't using his ex-wife quite as ruthlessly as her father had done.

"What could you possibly expect me to do at this point?" Ariston asked, wondering if she would be as truthful with him as her sister had been with her.

"*Expect?* Nothing." She sighed again, looking more defeated than anything else. "But *hope?* I guess I'm an irrepressible optimist, because I can't seem to give that commodity up entirely where you are concerned."

Again with the *hope* issue. What was it that she'd hoped for from him before and not gotten?

"And what is it you *hope?*" If she was as unwilling to answer this time as she had been the last, they would be at an impasse. For now.

"I'm not lending investment capital to a man who has no more business sense than to have kept the majority of his liquid assets in our home country's toppling banking institution," he said before she had a chance to answer his question.

Eber was a business dinosaur and his once thriving company had no chance with him at the helm in the new world economy, even without a powerful enemy like Ariston.

Chloe waited for their plates to be set before them before saying, "No, I can see that would be a mistake."

"If you do, you've gained business acumen you never had when married to me." He took a bite of his dinner, hoping it would encourage her to do the same and feeling triumphant when it worked.

The aged steak, seared but not cooked through, was one of the restaurant's specialty dishes he had always enjoyed. It did not disappoint, but Chloe looked equally pleased with her blackened salmon.

"I do understand some things," Chloe said after enjoying several thoughtful bites of her dinner. "Like the fact that Spiridakou & Sons Enterprises has weathered the current financial crisis in a way businesses in countries with much more stable economies than Greece have not."

"Though it may have started in Greece with my great-grandfather, SSE is now a fully functioning multinational corporation with headquarters in New York and Greece." He was proud of that fact.

His grandfather had made their company a multimillion-dollar concern. Ariston had taken it into the billions.

At thirty-two, he was one of the youngest billionaires living. Not entirely self-made, he'd nevertheless brought the company started by his great-grandfather to a level far beyond anything the Spiridakous that came before him had been able to achieve.

"Yes, with a brilliant businessman at its head." Chloe's voice was laced with unexpected approval and respect.

"You believe I am brilliant?"

"In business, there is no question." There was a caveat there in her voice.

He got the distinct impression, though, that if he asked about it, she would say it was nothing.

Or none of his business.

"So, what *do* you want?" he asked instead.

For a moment something poignant and vulnerable flared in her emerald gaze, but then it was gone. "My father signed over his principle interests in the company to my sister."

"Yes?" This was not news to Ariston.

Eber's health had deteriorated right along with his company. His move to make his daughter chairman had not been welcome, but Ariston had been determined to follow through with his plans no matter who spearheaded the Dioletis empire.

"You already knew that. Even so, you brought my father up. Twice." She shook her head. "You are such a shark."

# CHAPTER FOUR

"Guppies do not survive in my world."

"Don't remind me."

"You saw yourself as a guppy?" he couldn't help asking.

"Wouldn't you have, if you were me?"

When he just looked as if he couldn't imagine himself as anything but a predator, no matter the scenario, she went on. "Toward the end of our marriage, I came to realize how truly ill prepared I was to operate in your world, or that of my father for that matter."

"And yet, here you are again."

"Two years older and hopefully wiser."

"Did you know your father's health is not what it once was?" Ariston asked, realizing that if she hadn't spoken to the man in such a long while, she might not.

He couldn't be sure how far Rhea's honesty extended when dealing with Chloe.

"We've already established he's no longer at the helm of Dioletis Industries."

"That is not my point."

Chloe pushed her dinner away, having eaten about half of it. "What is your point?"

"I merely wished to make certain you knew of his ill health." Ariston frowned at the unfinished plate.

But Chloe didn't seem to notice. She was too busy looking askance at Ariston, her mouth twisted in confusion. "Why would you care?"

"Family is family."

"Which is why you see your parents so often." As digs went in the present circumstances, it was a good one.

"Neither of my parents are interested in relationships conducted on anything but their own terms." And Ariston was not a man to let others dictate the circumstances of his life.

He hadn't been since long before reaching his majority when he'd put a stop to the visitations with both parents in favor of attending boarding school in New York and spending holidays with his grandfather in Greece.

"So you should understand my estrangement with my father."

"I merely enquired as to whether you knew he was ill."

"Rhea told me as much. She said that was why he'd put her in charge of the company."

"But you were not sure whether or not to believe her."

"It was entirely possible Rhea was simply playing to my heartstrings. I'm not so naive that I don't realize my own sister has a good dose of business shark in herself as well. And she wants to save Dioletis Industries badly."

Chloe's expression turned troubled. "And I don't know how much of my father's illness is real and how much is contrived to manipulate Rhea into doing what he wanted. He felt a younger and more appealing face at the head of the company would have a positive effect on share prices."

Ariston let out a derisive sound.

"You know, there's something I don't understand."

"What is that?"

"Why you wouldn't speak to Rhea."

"I would think that would be obvious."

"You wanted to see me again," Chloe said with some resignation.

"Yes." He ate another bite of steak, but this time she didn't mirror his actions and he gave up, pushing his own plate away. "It is dangerously high blood pressure, I believe."

"What?"

"Your father's health issue."

Chloe's expression hardened. "I didn't ask."

"In light of his health, you do not feel the time has come to mend fences?"

"No."

"That is unlike you."

"As we established earlier, I've changed."

"Not in every way. You still find me irresistible."

"The feeling is mutual, it seemed to me," she said with some asperity.

He didn't deny it, but part of him would have liked to. Even if it would have been a lie. "Tell me what you want for Dioletis Industries."

"For hundreds of people to keep their jobs. For my sister not to end up having a heart attack before she's thirty."

"And you do not care how that happens?"

"Of course I care. What do you mean?"

He waved at her meal. "Eat. I didn't mean anything offensive. I merely wondered if maintaining the Dioletis name was important to you. I would guess not."

"Not for me, no." She made no move to eat.

Ah, but maybe it was for her sister, whom Chloe still spoke to and made no bones about loving despite their many differences. "What about Rhea?"

"She's willing to offer up enough stock to make you majority shareholder, if that's what you're asking," Chloe said after they'd eaten in silence for a few minutes. "Frankly, I can't imagine a better outcome."

He kept his surprise at that pronouncement off his face. "In exchange for how large an infusion of cash?"

Rhea had been right to assume he would insist on being made a majority shareholder before he gave the Dioletis empire another fifty cents. Those shares would preferably come from Eber, but Ariston wouldn't quibble about the source, merely the final outcome.

He was pleasantly surprised that Rhea was already in the right headspace for the deal he meant to propose though.

"I don't know."

"You do not know?"

"No. I told you, I don't have anything to do with the company now. Rhea said you would know what needed doing and if you were willing to do it, would set the terms."

"Rhea's a smart woman."

"Yes."

"And if my terms included taking most or all of your sister's stock?" he asked, giving no indication whether her answer would make any difference to him.

"That sounds more like a hostile takeover than a bail-out or a merger, but I don't have any doubts Rhea would go for it," Chloe said, making no effort to hide how desperate Rhea was to save the company.

"No doubts at all?"

"No. She's willing to have the company absorbed by SSE if that's what it takes to keep people employed, and anything that gets my sister out from under the two-ton weight she's got on her shoulders right now is a good idea to me."

"I doubt Rhea would thank you for telling me either of

those things." Not that knowing them made any difference to the outcome.

He had already decided what was going to happen.

"Right now, my sister is fighting to save her marriage and a company that's going down the drain faster than water. She's not going to quibble how she manages either."

"Her marriage?" He knew Eber had not approved of Samuel, but Rhea had always seemed smitten.

"Samuel is sick of coming second to the company and Rhea's had two miscarriages already. The doctor said if she continues working under such stressful conditions, her chances of a viable pregnancy are almost nil."

"She could have allowed someone else to take over the chairmanship."

"Not according to my father." Chloe's tone was laced with a more intense form of the same anger she'd shown toward Eber Dioletis every time his name was mentioned.

"Rhea is an adult. She makes her own choices," Ariston pointed out.

"Some choices are harder to make than others."

"Like moving across the country and starting a new life."

"That one wasn't so hard."

"I think perhaps you have a streak of ruthlessness."

Chloe's lovely green eyes widened and she shook her head. "No."

"You left Greece without looking back."

Her face spasmed with emotion. "We aren't discussing the end of our marriage."

"No, apparently you're more interested in seeing that your sister's marriage doesn't suffer a similar fate."

"Yes." This time Chloe's tone was filled with a wealth of emotion. Her shoulders slumped. "I hate seeing her so stressed. Samuel makes her happy, he makes her feel loved and wanted, but she's going to lose him for the sake of my father's approval and the *company.*"

"It's a pity you didn't take our marriage as seriously as you take your sister's."

"It was an entirely different circumstance."

"Really? You certainly maintained a happy facade during our marriage. I would not have considered you an actress capable of keeping up that kind of subterfuge for three years."

"I…that's not important any longer."

"No, your sister's happiness is all that matters."

"Hundreds of employees and their families matter, too," Chloe said with complete earnestness.

"Once again, you are not thinking of yourself." Which was something his plans counted on, so he wasn't complaining. Merely observing.

"I'm not important in this."

"You'd be surprised." He asked, "Do you want your sister to maintain a directorial position with the company?"

He didn't see Rhea happy as a homemaker and Chloe had stated her sister's happiness was at the forefront of her priorities.

"She's willing to step down completely, but is hoping you'll keep her on in a managerial capacity. I'm hoping it will be a position with more normal hours and stress levels." Chloe gave him a beseeching look. "Rhea's smart. You know that. She's got her MBA from Harvard. She has impressive contacts and if our father had stepped down five years ago, maybe the company wouldn't be where it is today."

Perhaps, but then again, perhaps not. Chloe was wholly unaware of Ariston's moves behind the scenes and for now, he was content to keep it that way.

"She has more in common with your father than with you, Chloe, no matter what you'd like to think."

Chloe surprised him by nodding in quick agreement. "But she's not *just* like him, and for her sake as well as the people who love her, I don't want to see Rhea become any more like Eber Dioletis than she is."

"I think you are seeing a softness that isn't there." The woman had refused to leave her job despite the fact that the stress levels and long work hours had resulted in multiple miscarriages.

"No. It's there. She cares about people. Samuel. Me. She saved my life."

"What do you mean?"

Chloe looked away, an expression of shame flitting across her features. "It doesn't matter—all that matters is that I'm here because she deserves for me to be."

"And if you want me to listen to your pleas on her behalf, you'll tell me why I should."

"My reasons won't matter to you."

"I'll be the judge of that, Chloe."

"I stopped eating after I left Greece. Not on purpose, or anything, but food just didn't appeal."

"Why?"

Chloe shrugged. "Reaction to ending our marriage, I guess."

"It was your choice." But it certainly didn't seem as if she'd enjoyed making it.

"Like I said before, some choices are harder than others."

"And yet you made it."

"I did."

"But you stopped eating," he prompted, wanting to understand how that could have gotten life-threatening.

Though looking at how thin she was two years on, maybe he already had his answer.

"Yes. I didn't even really notice when I started losing weight. Rhea did and she went ballistic on me, insisting I see a nutritional counselor. She wanted me to go to the therapist, but relented when I changed my eating habits and gained back a bit of weight."

"This is you after gaining some weight back?" he asked in shock. "How much had you lost?"

"More than I could afford and maintain my health." The stubborn tilt to his ex-wife's chin said she wasn't going into more detail.

"What did your father think of all this?"

"I have no idea. Rhea respected my decision to cut ties with him."

"Even though that must have caused problems between the two of them."

"I'm sure it did, but Rhea never taxed me with it."

"You're very loyal to each other."

"Yes." Chloe's eyes shone with unmistakable emotion.

He understood that sort of loyalty, probably better than most. He would do anything for his grandfather.

"You are saying you grieved the end of our marriage."

"Of course I did."

There was no *of course,* but they would get to that in due time.

"I find it hard to believe that you do not care if Dioletis Industries ceases to exist." He knew Chloe wasn't as enamored of the business as her father and sister, but no matter what she said, it *was* her heritage.

"As long as people stay employed? No." Sincerity rang in Chloe's voice. "One way or another, Dioletis Industries has taken more from me than I could afford to give."

"What do you mean?" He was learning things about his ex-wife he'd had no clue about in the three years of their marriage.

"It always had *all* of my father's attention. Though I truly believed he loved my mother, he neglected her. I was only eleven when she died, but I was old enough to have seen the impact my father's priorities had on Mom. He hurt her time and again. And she always forgave him."

"He hurt you, too, the daughter more interested in art than business, unlike Rhea," he surmised.

Chloe nodded and then sighed. "That's water under the bridge, just like my degree in fine arts. I'm really not interested in discussing my father, his company, or the past. Since Rhea holds voting privileges for majority stock in Dioletis Industries, whatever she wants to happen to the company is what is going to happen."

Eber could still kick up a fuss by revoking his proxy from his daughter, but by the time the paperwork cleared, Ariston's acquisition of his company would already have gone through. Possession was considered nine-tenths of the law by most people. For a Spiridakou? *It was the law.*

He wasn't giving up what was his. Not even his ex-wife.

"You do not expect to get anything out of this deal personally?" he asked, knowing the answer even as he did so.

"No."

It was so damn Chloe, and so not a woman who would enter a contract with the intent to defraud the other party. He'd allowed himself to forget the woman he had spent three years living with and replaced her in his mind with a caricature that did not fit Chloe Spiridakou at all.

Even the Chloe Spiridakou who had lied and used birth control to circumvent their original contract. There were motivations here he still did not understand, but he would.

It was in his nature to keep at a problem until he had it solved. Something told him he'd just begun to scratch the surface of the problem of the woman he'd married.

His plans would give him all the time he needed to dig deeper.

"And if I want something personal?" he asked smoothly.

For several long seconds, Chloe could do nothing but gape at her ex-husband. This is what all the questions were leading to, and the sex, and probably even the specially flavored coffee! He'd been setting her up.

Because he wanted something from her. He'd already gotten the sex. What else could it be? Maybe he wanted more?

"You're saying you want something *personally,* for you?" she asked, clarifying.

"I'm saying I want something personal for me *from you.*"

Well, there could be no mistaking his intention with those words. "But what exactly?"

She still couldn't fathom anything he could possibly want from her that he couldn't get with a lot less effort and money than it would take to save Dioletis Industries.

"What if I were to tell you that I want something similar to the agreement five years ago?"

"Is that what you're telling me?" she asked, not sure she could believe what her ears were telling her.

He'd had the divorce papers drawn up and ready for use, not her. And he'd made absolutely zero effort to contact her after she walked out of their apartment in Athens. She might have left him, but he'd shown no interest in getting her back.

And she was just now realizing how much she'd been hoping he would.

*"Ne."* Definite. Affirmative. And in Greek.

He meant business. Literally.

"You want to marry me again?" Shock coursed through her and made her voice break.

It was quickly followed by sick dread as her imagination ran wild. Maybe he wanted to try the business-arrangement marriage again, but this time with her sister? And he needed Chloe to help him convince Rhea.

Only, hadn't she made it clear that she was meeting him in the first place because ultimately Chloe wanted to see her sister's marriage saved? Not destroyed by another business deal meant to save Dioletis Industries.

Ariston had said he knew everything about his business interests; perhaps he'd known about the cracks in Rhea's marriage before even Chloe. And was counting on them?

They'd always gotten along, Rhea and Ariston. They had so much in common. More than she and Ariston had ever had.

Would Rhea do it? Marry Chloe's ex, if it meant saving their father's empire? She wouldn't give Samuel up for the company, would she? Only a sinking feeling in Chloe's gut said that Rhea just might.

She'd darn near done it already.

"Chloe...*yineka mou*...are you well?" Suddenly Ariston was there. Squatting in his sharply tailored suit and fresh shirt beside her dining chair.

His hand cupped her cheek oh so carefully, his cerulean eyes filled with a concern she knew she couldn't let herself believe in.

"What is the matter?" he demanded.

She almost laughed, but was afraid if she started, she wouldn't stop until the tears came. "You said...marry..."

And her brain had taken wing to a dark, ugly place, Chloe never, ever, *ever* wanted to live.

"*Not* marriage...not exactly."

"Not exactly." *Not with Rhea?* "What then, *exactly?*"

His hand dropped, but he remained where he was, his gaze boring into hers. "I want you in my bed."

It didn't even surprise her that he'd said it out loud in the middle of the restaurant. He wasn't speaking loud enough for his voice to carry far, but she didn't think it would matter to him if he had been.

Ariston didn't live by normal people's rules.

"I…that…" He wanted a mistress? A lover? What?

*"Without the birth control,"* he said with intense conviction. "I want the baby you withheld from me."

*"You knew."* Shock upon shock. She'd been so sure he wasn't aware.

She couldn't even begin to deal with his comment about a baby just that second.

"I told you." He stood and returned to his seat. Still close, but a vast gulf of emotion and understanding between them. "There is very little about my business interests that I do not know."

"I never felt like a business interest when we were together," she said helplessly, her mind reeling. "Not until the end and I saw you planned to divorce me just as the contract said you could after three years and still keep the stocks."

He said nothing, his silence speaking words she didn't want to hear.

She shook her head, but her thoughts refused to settle as they spun endlessly around one simple fact. "I don't understand how you *could* know."

"I found your pills."

"In my jewelry armoire?" But he never went through her things.

Only he must have. At least once.

"Yes."

"Why?"

"Does it matter?"

"Maybe it shouldn't…but I feel like it does." If he had never trusted her and had *spied* on her, that put their marriage in a different light, even for her, didn't it?

"I was planning a gift for you."

"And you needed something in my jewelry armoire?" she asked with a fatalistic sense of doom.

"Yes."

"When?"

"Is that really important?"

"Probably not." The fact that he had known was the only thing that really mattered.

Because somehow she was beyond certain his discovery of the packet of pills had led to those divorce papers being drawn up. The only question she didn't have an answer for was, why had he waited to have the papers served?

But then maybe she had her answer already—in their contract, the clause that stipulated he had to wait until they'd been married exactly three years to divorce her, or forfeit the stocks in Dioletis Industries.

Suddenly the whys and wherefores of his discovery and what she thought it had led to faded into the background as the full implication of his words hit.

*"You want me to give you a child."* The horrified shock she felt infused every word and she made no effort to hide it.

His brows drew together as if her response puzzled him, but he said, "Yes."

"I won't do it." She shook her head adamantly and then went to take a fortifying sip of the wine she'd ordered with dinner, only to have the glass shake so badly in her trembling fingers she was forced to give it up. "I won't."

His blue gaze narrowed, both his expression and tone taking on a calculating cast. "Not even for your sister and all of those employees you supposedly care so much about?"

"You would have me give up my own child in order to save other families?" she hissed across the table at him with a depth of pain she hadn't realized he was still capable of drawing forth in her.

"You would not want to give up your child?" he asked, as if curious in a merely academic way.

The jerk. The world-class, *professional* jerk.

"Surely you know me well enough to know that?" She'd accepted he knew her with far less intimacy than she'd sought to know him, but this was ludicrous.

Even the postman knew Chloe well enough to know she'd never give up her child. Well, okay, maybe not. But the principle was true anyway.

"It is not something one can simply make assumptions about."

"I'm not your mother, Ariston. She and your father are both idiots, if you want my opinion." It was one she'd never voiced during their marriage, but really?

That generation of Spiridakous were a mess and Ariston had to realize it. He had almost nothing to do with them himself.

That didn't mean he enjoyed hearing her say it out loud.

He went stern on her. "I did not ask for it."

"No, you merely judged me by standards of behavior they set. You know me…or at least you did. You have to know that's not something I could do." She took a deep breath, but it didn't help the anxiety building inside her. "I just can't."

"I came to realize that I did not know you at all."

He for sure hadn't, if he could suggest something so monstrous. Something that no matter the incentive she would not, or rather *could not* do.

Standing on shaky legs, she shook her head again, not wanting to look at him, but equally incapable of looking anywhere else. "No. I won't do it."

# CHAPTER FIVE

FEELING as if she was starring in her own one-act tragedy, Chloe headed out of the restaurant.

How could he expect her to give up their child? Not only a part of her, but a part of *him?*

Her eyes burned, her throat going tight. She hadn't hurt this much since the day she'd left Greece.

Even the day their divorce had become final, her grief had been muted by the knowledge she'd had no choice but to leave and the divorce had been inevitable.

His having the papers drawn up had been irrefutable proof to her that no matter how hot the sex between them, no matter how tenderly he sometimes treated her, the reality was that Ariston had seen her as nothing but a business deal. When she'd finally really accepted that, she'd known she had to walk away before she lost herself as her mother had done.

Only she'd now learned that her own actions had precipitated one of the most painful moments of her life— reading those coldly precise divorce papers.

She'd thought she was protecting herself, but in reality she'd undermined her own chances with the man she loved.

She *knew* how his brain worked. He would have decided she was a cheat, an operator out for what she could get without giving what she promised.

*She* knew she had every intention of giving the Spiridakous the heir they were so keen on—just not until he admitted he wanted her for more than three years. But he wouldn't have assumed any such thing.

He did not have a trusting nature.

Realizing Ariston had discovered her use of birth control gave their entire marriage and the end of it a different interpretation. She'd said it didn't matter when he'd found out, but realized that it did.

Very much.

Had he known from day one? Nausea rolled through her at the prospect.

He hadn't said so, but she knew Ariston had to have been beyond furious once he'd learned of the birth control. And yet, she'd never even guessed he knew.

Either Ariston was an amazing prevaricator…or she'd meant so little to him that even what he would have seen as betrayal didn't impact how he treated her.

Not that *that* would be a surprise. Not anymore.

However, the knowledge that he'd had sex with her—repeatedly—while thinking she was a cheat and a liar made her body clammy with sweat as the nausea made her stomach cramp.

His emotions had *never* been engaged with her. Not even a little. Not even when she'd been so sure they were.

She remembered a party they'd attended together toward the end of their marriage. They'd gone because Ariston wanted to make a business contact. He'd even said so.

But when she'd come down from their bedroom dressed in a teal sheath that dipped with a sexy cowl in the back and hugged her curves in all the right places, Ariston's eyes had heated with something she'd been sure at the time was more than lust.

\* \* \*

"You look beautiful tonight."

Chloe smiled up at her husband, her heart rate jumping at the look in his gorgeous cerulean eyes. "Thank you. You clean up pretty nicely yourself."

He looked amazing in his tailored tuxedo.

"I wish we didn't have this party to go to tonight."

His words shocked and thrilled her and Chloe beamed. "Maybe we won't stay too late?"

"Maybe they'll be lucky if we remain through the appetizers," he growled as he kissed her with a tender passion he'd been showing more and more lately.

"Your grandfather called and wants us at his house in Piraeus this weekend," she said after reapplying her lipstick and straightening his black silk bowtie.

"He adores you and it is easy to understand why. You are good to him."

"I'm good to you, too," she teased.

Ariston grinned, the smile reaching his eyes as it didn't with most people. "Yes, *yineka mou,* you are."

On the way to the party, he surprised her with a very special gift. "I've arranged for you to take drawing lessons from…" He named an eminent artist Chloe would have been in awe over meeting, much less taking any sort of lesson from.

"I didn't know he went in for private tutoring."

"He does not."

"But he made an exception for you," she guessed.

"He made the exception for you, my very precious wife."

They didn't even stay at the party long enough for the main course to be set out on the buffet. Ariston missed the opportunity to talk to the businessman he'd intended to meet, but had dismissed Chloe's concerns with a wave of his hand as he ushered her out of the crowded mansion. "Some things are more important than business."

In that moment Chloe had believed she was one of them.

When she'd learned the contrary, the emotional devastation had left her existing in a wasteland that nearly cost her health.

Coming back into the present, Chloe felt her knees buckle and she stumbled, bumping into a man on the sidewalk. He said something to her, but she didn't hear him.

She was too focused inward.

He grabbed her arm and shouted something about snotty rich bitches thinking they owned the sidewalks. She raised her head, thinking she needed to apologize, but she didn't get the chance.

Ariston was there, yanking the man away, his bodyguards closing in to put a protective barrier between Chloe and everyone else.

Warm hands cupped her face. "You're freezing." He cursed in Greek and English. "You're in shock."

She didn't say anything, just stared at him while too many thoughts vied for her attention. She had no hope of grasping hold of any single one of them.

"So, the prospect of having a child does this to you. Even now? Or is it the thought of having *my* child?"

"It's not that," she denied, her voice made weak by her distress, but the emotion behind her words vehement enough to make her brain work again. "I can't believe you found…" She shook her head. "You would have been *so angry.*"

"I was livid," he admitted, a muscle ticking in his jaw. "No man likes to be played the fool."

Especially not a business shark like him. "No. You wouldn't. But I never knew."

"I guess we both were good at hiding things."

"How good was I?" She needed to know. She didn't care if he thought it mattered. It did to her.

"What do you mean?"

"When did you find out?" she asked, only now realizing he'd been moving her toward a limousine with its back door open the whole time they'd been talking.

He tried to usher her inside, but she balked. "Tell me."

"A month before we left New York."

"No..." It was almost funny in a macabre kind of way.

Because by then, she'd decided even if it was a baby holding them together it was worth keeping her marriage to the man she loved with her whole heart. She'd stopped taking her pills almost a month before that, but hadn't gotten pregnant.

She wasn't sure at first, though—those first two weeks after returning to the States she'd lived in a state of dread. The idea of staying married to him under the circumstances had been untenable. Not only that, but the contract hadn't specified what happened if she had a baby *after* the marriage ended.

All custody parameters might have been negated by her timing.

She climbed into the limo without further protest, her movements clumsy and awkward.

They'd driven in silence for several minutes when he made a sound of exasperation. "I did not say you would have to give up our child. You are the one who suggested it."

He still believed that's what she was upset about? She was. Really upset. The very idea horrified her. But even such a despicable plan paled in comparison to the knowledge that her effort to protect herself had been the reason she lost her marriage and the love of her life.

She tried to tell herself it had been for the best. What kind of life would they have had together with him caring so little for her?

More memories of the life they had shared flashed through her mind, taunting her with how happy she'd been. Yes, there had been moments of pain, days she'd despaired in her unrequited love, but there'd been so many more when she'd simply been blissfully happy.

It was no use trying to deny it. She would have taken *that* life and with gratitude.

Two years on, she was no longer convinced love on one side wasn't enough. Not when the other side respected their marriage vows and provided the kind of passion in intimacy that most women only dreamed about.

Okay, so he hadn't adored her, or anything like that, but he'd been kind to her—when he remembered she existed. No question his position with SSE had come first, but she'd never expected anything different.

Yes, it hurt to love unrequited, but Chloe now knew how much more it hurt to walk away from that love. Especially when his lack of emotional commitment to her had not shown itself until she'd read those divorce papers.

Ariston had done marriage really well.

She couldn't change the past, though. No matter how much she might want to. She couldn't say, "Oops, maybe I should have waited to walk out."

Even now, knowing everything, she was still fairly certain she'd done the right thing.

She dashed at eyes now spilling. She had to get herself together. And get out of this limousine.

He made an exasperated sound and she looked up at him.

"Stop looking so damn tragic. If you become pregnant and carry my child to term successfully, I will marry you."

*"What?"* Nothing was making sense here. He had not just offered her the world on a platter. Him and a baby, too. "You said *not* marriage."

"I told you, a modification of our original agreement."

"That agreement was never between you and me." And hadn't that been part of the problem? "We were our family's pawns."

"I do not play chess, Chloe. You know this. I will never play the pawn." He reclined against the opposite seat, his body's relaxed pose belied by the tension in his blue eyes.

"But you only married me because your grandfather wanted great-grandchildren."

"Considering all that he has done for me, is it so strange I should seek to give him what he wants? Even now?"

So, it was *still* about his grandfather. She could not be surprised. The fact that Ariston wanted Chloe to be the mother of the grandchild he was determined to provide the old man *was,* however.

"You are so sure *I* would be willing to marry *you* in that case?" Even she didn't know what she'd do in that case.

"You will sign an ironclad contract to that effect, one that will guarantee you lose primary custody of our child should you refuse to do so," he said with the air of a man who had recently discovered his biggest bargaining chip and had no hesitations about using it.

"I—"

"Come, you know you were content enough to be my wife before. In certain cases, even passionately so." The look he gave her said he referred to their incredible compatibility in the bedroom. "Do not deny it. You walked out because you thought I planned to divorce you. This is our chance at a do-over."

"You did plan to divorce me, and I walked out because our marriage was a business sham."

"Our marriage was more compatible than any I've seen based on so-called love."

"Rhea and Samuel—"

"Are on the brink of divorce."

She couldn't deny it. "But there are loads of people who are happily married and love each other."

"Not in our world."

"Even in our world. What about Leiandros Kiriakis and his wife, Savannah? They've been married for nearly a decade and are still very much in love."

"You barely know them. You only see the surface of their relationship."

"It's real. The love between them is real." Even knowing them as little as she did, she couldn't doubt it. "Besides, they aren't the only ones. There's Demitri and Alexandra Petronides. You remember the scandal around their marriage, but they weathered the storm and are still very much in love."

Ariston frowned. "We aren't talking about our acquaintances right now, Chloe. We have things far more personal to discuss."

"What is more personal than love?"

"For us? A great deal."

She stared at him, trying to understand why he was so against the concept of marital love. His parents had a lot to answer for, she knew, but after what he'd shared in the restaurant, she wondered if Shannon might have even more to do with it.

But if he wanted to focus on them, that's what she'd do. "If I had been content, I never would have left Athens without you."

"Your father instigated that, and now I have to wonder if he didn't do it on purpose."

A shard of pain went through her heart as Chloe realized how very real that possibility was. Her father had made his plans and her marriage wasn't going to stand in the way. "It doesn't matter. He didn't make up the divorce papers. *You* had them drawn up."

"Surely you expected nothing else. You prevented any hope of our marriage lasting beyond the three years by preventing the conception of my child."

She'd come to that conclusion herself and found it no less palatable having him say it aloud. "I did not think you would stick to the letter of the contract."

"Why should I do anything else?"

No reason. Certainly not because he loved her and needed her in his life, or anything. She swallowed back any reply she might want to make and turned her face toward the window.

He sighed from the other side of the car. "I had the papers drawn in a fit of rage, but I would not have served you with them without clarifying matters between us first."

That got her attention back on him. "What?"

"Unlike you, I had no intention of throwing away our marriage without first finding out why you'd been using the birth control."

"When I left, that must have made it look like I'd never had any intention of fulfilling the contract."

"Yes."

She swallowed, accepting her responsibility for that. "You wanted to stay married?"

"As I said, we were compatible."

"But you were very angry I'd circumvented the contract, weren't you?"

"Beyond angry. I went to Hong Kong to establish some distance."

"I had no idea."

"That was intentional."

"But why? If you were going to talk to me, why not do it right away?"

"I was too furious. You did not merely betray me, you betrayed my grandfather as well."

"I didn't intend to betray either of you."

He made a noncommittal sound.

"Why me…I mean, this time around? There are lots of women who would be glad to give you a child."

He shrugged as if all those other women didn't matter. "You have something I want and I have something you need."

"My family's company needs, you mean." She laughed, the sound nothing like humorous. "If all you want is a womb, more than half the planet's population has one."

*"Pappous."*

His grandfather? What did Takis Spiridakou have to do with anything?

"You cannot tell me Takis will be happy for you to marry the mother of your child *after* its birth." The old man was a traditional Greek in the best sense of the words.

"My grandfather does not recognize the American divorce decree, despite the fact we were legally married here in New York."

Ah. So, it had to be her. Because Takis Spiridakou was not a man who considered the laws of a nation supreme to those of his church.

"We married in the Orthodox church." They'd had a second, far more elaborate ceremony in Greece. Both their families had been in attendance for it, unlike their civil ceremony in New York for legalities' sake.

And in the eyes of the Spiridakou family patriarch, that made her and Ariston's marriage sacred and permanent.

The old man's stubbornness almost brought a real smile

to her lips. She loved the old Greek as much as if he'd been her own grandfather.

"He considers our vows sacred." Ariston said, echoing her thoughts. "According to Pappous, you are still my wife."

"What does he think of the bed partners you've had since I left Greece?" she wondered aloud.

Takis would not have approved of infidelity.

Ariston's lips quirked with amusement. "I assure you, I do not discuss my sex life with my grandfather."

Which was not an answer to what she was really asking, but then that was fair, she told herself. After all, Ariston had never claimed that *he* believed them still married despite the divorce decree.

"Has it been a very active one since I left?" she heard herself asking without having given her mouth permission to speak.

"To quote a woman I know, none of your business."

*"Bastard."* Her hand flew to cover her mouth.

She *never* used language like that, and honestly, she hadn't even called him that in her own mind. But having him throw her own words back at her right now sent her irritation levels right through the roof of the limo.

Ariston didn't take offense. In fact, he laughed. "You wouldn't be the first to think so."

Her ex-husband in business mode was dangerous enough, but when he reverted to charming and approachable? Perfectly fatal to her heart.

"Let me get this straight," she said, needing to get the topic of the conversation back on track. "You'll refrain from selling your shares in Dioletis Industries and provide the infusion of capital necessary as well as the savvy business direction to keep it solvent if I play the part of your mistress for an indefinite period of time until I fall pregnant?"

Saying it aloud made it sound a lot more worrisome than the concept had in her mind. Not to mention, unbelievable.

Even considering his grandfather's stubborn attitude about their dissolved marriage, Ariston didn't need to negotiate to have her in his bed. He'd already proven that this afternoon.

Yes, there was the child issue, she supposed. For him, that was clearly the bigger one.

"*Mistress* is an old-fashioned term that implies I have other conjugal responsibilities. I do not. You would be my lover, and should you get pregnant—"

"And carry the baby to term." They couldn't forget that little gem of a caveat.

"*Ne*. Yes, and give birth to my child..."

"I would then be expected to marry you," she finished for him.

He nodded. "And should you be tempted to renegotiate terms at that time, we will have the aforementioned iron-clad contract, witnessed in both New York and Athens, in place."

"And presumably, I will sign this contract for the sake of the hundreds of employees of Dioletis Industries and their families that would be adversely affected if you don't do your business voodoo with Dioletis Industries."

"And your sister. You've said you would do anything to help her save her marriage and maintain her own happiness. This is your opportunity to prove the veracity of your words."

Wow. So, yeah...they'd never really been in the same place. She was convinced that since reaching adulthood, and probably a good time before that, *this* man had never been as vulnerable to someone else's whims as Chloe had at twenty.

"Doesn't it bother you to take advantage of someone else like this?" And how different from her father was Ariston really if he could do it so easily?

There was no mistaking the look of offense sliding over his features. "You'll become the wife of a billionaire. I do not see where that is *taking advantage*."

The man really was too arrogant for words.

"Right. What's yet another relationship between us without love?"

"Again with the love thing? Understand this—I do not believe in it."

"Why not?" She had her own ideas about it, but wanted to hear his own words on the subject.

"I have seen too much evidence that *love* makes the worst basis possible for marriage. My father has claimed to love every one of his six wives, and my mother *loves* every man she takes to her bed. Love is at best an excuse to follow one's libido. A contract, when each side cannot mistake the terms, is a much better basis for marriage."

"Wow." Cynical much? Though she really couldn't blame him. "Not everyone loves like your parents." And the contract thing sure hadn't worked for them the first time around.

Though if she were to say that, she had no doubt he'd blame her for subverting the terms.

"Shannon claimed to love me and I was certain that I loved her, but when I discovered her perfidy, I was far more angry than hurt."

Chloe had no doubt Ariston had loved the schemer, because the relationship had had way too big an impact on him for anything but real emotion. She didn't contradict him, though.

She found the idea of trying to convince Ariston he had in fact loved another woman nausea-producing.

Regardless, considering his views on the subject, she didn't think bringing up her love for him would help their current situation, or dialogue.

She knew Ariston loved his grandfather. Maybe the old Greek was the only person Ariston was capable of feeling such a tender emotion toward nowadays.

He had no affectionate feelings for his parents that she'd ever been able to discern. Not that they had done anything to engender even a mild liking. Balios and Evia Spiridakou were sociopathically selfish and always had been from everything she'd heard. They were certainly worse than neglectful parents to Ariston.

The American socialite and the Greek playboy had divorced when Ariston was young, splitting custody equally between them. He'd grown up living half the year in New York and half the year in Athens. The latter half was better, according to Ariston, because he'd spent those months living in his grandfather's home with his father popping in and out like a self-centered genie.

Ariston had never shared what he'd suffered because of them, but he'd told Chloe once that the only place he felt safe as a child was with his grandfather.

They arrived at their destination and she realized it was her hotel. Despite their family's dwindling coffers, her sister had booked Chloe in at a five-star hotel. Rhea was insistent that appearances had to be maintained for the sake of the business.

Ariston moved as if to exit the car with her. "I'll see you inside. We still have much to discuss."

If he came up to her room, they might well talk, but she wasn't naive enough to believe that was all that would happen. "Right. First payments on the contract," she offered flippantly before stepping out of the car.

He took her arm and led her into the Park Avenue entrance. "Wouldn't that have been this afternoon?"

"I didn't know about your proposition then, so how could it?" she asked as her heels clicked an angry tattoo across the marble floor of the lobby.

Not that this evening could be either, since she hadn't actually agreed to what he was proposing.

She wasn't entirely sure she was going to allow things to end up in bed, but she wasn't sure she wouldn't either. She felt like an accident victim...shocky and in need of physical connection. He was here, and if she could choose to be held by anyone, no matter how odd it might seem, Ariston was at the top of her list at present.

He wouldn't have been, even a day ago.

How had things changed so quickly? Or had they not changed at all, only her willingness to admit to them—if only to herself?

"No, you did not," he said as he guided her into the elevator. "Why *did* you have sex with me? Maybe it was your version of falling at my feet on behalf of the Dioletis Industries employees. Considering how explosive we always were in bed, it wasn't a bad strategy."

She spun to face him. "I wasn't the one who started it!"

"No, but you made no objections once I did. I have to wonder why."

"Are you really that insecure? Because you are the dead-sexiest man I've ever met. Is that plain-speaking enough for you?" She turned away.

Idiot. He was such a corporate shark, he couldn't think of any reason for sex other than a business ploy. He probably *had* made the move on her in order to influence her response to his proposition. She could hardly deny now that she still wanted him, but she wouldn't have anyway.

"I'm glad to hear it."

"I'm sure you are."

When they reached her room, she silently let him inside.

Ariston sighed. "I had no ulterior motives for what happened earlier in my office either. I have never made a secret of how much I enjoy your body."

Some of the tension drained from Chloe. At least he hadn't been trying to manipulate her with sex. That would have just felt so darn tawdry—and frankly, his proposal was bad enough.

She put her purse away in the armoire and slipped out of heels she hadn't worn in two years before today. She'd changed from her suit earlier to a simple black dress that had once been her favorite for dinner.

Now all she wanted was out of it and into comfy clothes for this discussion, but that wasn't going to happen. "Takis is a very stubborn man. He hasn't even seen me in two years."

"Not by his choice."

She jerked around to face Ariston, who stood in the middle of the simple guest room, watching her intently.

"He wanted to see me?" she demanded.

The old man had called a few times, but Chloe had found their conversations painful and ducked his calls for the most part. He'd never mentioned wanting to come visit in any of their brief phone calls. He'd also never said anything about the fact he still considered her and Ariston married, though he had mentioned she was still his granddaughter. Perhaps the old man felt the former went without saying.

"He did."

As far as she knew, the older man had never stepped off

his native Greek soil. "He wanted to *come to the States, to see me?*"

Ariston inclined his head in agreement.

"But you prevented him."

At that he laughed, just as he'd done when they were married...when she'd thought they were happy. "No one tells Pappous what to do. His health prevented him."

"Or what to think, apparently. So he really still considers me your wife?" she asked with a slight smile, tickled by the old man's intransigence.

"He considers our divorce a youthful indiscretion on my part."

"I was the one who walked out." She didn't feel like smiling anymore. "And you were thirty, hardly a youth."

Despite what his grandfather claimed, Ariston had been fully cognizant of what he was doing.

"It is my grandfather's perspective," Ariston said with a shrug. "To bring him joy in his final years, I would do much."

"Final years?"

"He is not a young man."

"You said he had problems with his health. What kind?" she asked, unable to keep the question back now her worry for the old man was growing.

"He's been diagnosed with Parkinson's. He's responding to treatment, but his age complicates things." Both regret and determination laced Ariston's tone.

Chloe reached out and laid her hand over his heart. "I'm sorry. He's a very special person. I've missed him."

It wasn't hard to admit. Chloe and Takis had been close.

"As am I." Ariston covered her hand with his own, his eyes for once revealing his thoughts with almost pure transparency.

Ariston was hurting and he felt helpless. He wanted to

give his grandfather the one thing he'd ever asked Ariston for, an heir to their empire. Another grandchild to love as he had loved Ariston.

Realizing that he might well be feeling the same need for physical closeness she was, if for wholly different reasons, she reached up to kiss him.

He drew her close, taking over the kiss and showing her just how close he wanted to get physically.

# CHAPTER SIX

CHLOE woke the next morning to the sound of rustling movement. Her eyes fluttered open and she saw Ariston leaning over his briefcase he'd propped on the room's desk.

She blinked at the alarm clock on the bedside table and groaned. "You always were an early riser."

He looked over his shoulder. "You are awake."

"And you've already showered." She tugged the sheet to her chest and sat up in the bed. "Are you leaving?"

"We still have a few things to discuss." He turned to face her completely and she noticed he held a thick, bound document.

The cover was red with Spiridakous & Sons Enterprises logo in the center.

"What is that?" she asked.

He handed it to Chloe. "Tell your sister she has forty-eight hours to accept or decline the terms outlined here."

"Aren't you taking a lot for granted?" She hadn't agreed to his proposition.

"Am I?" He looked pointedly at the rumpled bed sheets. "You didn't balk at the terms of my deal last night."

"Last night wasn't about the deal."

"Wasn't it?"

She glared up at him. "No."

"Are you turning me down?"

"Is that what last night was? You trying to convince me?"

"I've made no secret of the fact that I want you back in my bed."

"And a baby for your grandfather's old age."

Ariston shrugged, the prospectus in his hand a red beacon forcing her to face the reality of what he was both offering and asking.

Was Chloe going to do it? Was she going to agree to his terms, return to his bed…to the agreement they made five years ago? Give him the child she'd intended to the first time around?

She'd walked out on him because she'd thought he didn't value their marriage, never mind not return her love. She'd been wrong, though. He had valued their marriage. Even though he'd believed her guilty of circumventing the contract, Ariston had intended to talk to her before divorcing her.

Would he have followed through with the divorce after she admitted why she'd put off getting pregnant? With his attitude toward love, her confession might actually have tipped him toward filing the papers rather than having them shredded.

They would never know what would have happened two years ago if they'd talked out his anger and her worries, but they had a chance at a new future now.

Did she want to take it? Did she have a choice? If she turned him down, Rhea and the employees of Dioletis Industries would all pay the price.

"Chloe?" Ariston prompted.

"Just thinking."

"About my offer?" he asked.

"Yes. And the past."

"The past has little bearing on the present."

"I think you're wrong." She'd walked away from him

and with her best efforts, admitted—if only to herself—
that the life she'd been living the past two years had been
muted.

Dulled by grief at losing her best chance at love, drained
of the sparkle being around a man as dynamic as Ariston
had given to her days.

"I made a life for myself," she said softly. "It's not
empty." It really wasn't. Not as exciting as her life with
him, but absolutely not without its own benefits. "I have
friends, an occupation I find both interesting and chal-
lenging, a position within my community."

"But you do not have me."

"You talk like you think I love you."

The familiar look of derision at the mention of that
word came over his features, but then it morphed into a
smile. "You enjoyed our life together. You enjoyed being
my wife."

"And yet I walked away from it."

"Why?" he asked, sitting on the side of the bed, his intense focus wholly on her in a way it rarely had ever been
except when making love. "You said we wanted different
things. You thought I wanted a divorce."

"I wanted love," she admitted, thinking this might well
be the moment he tossed that red folio back into his briefcase and walked out of the hotel room.

"We had something better than love."

"Only you would think a contract made up for an emotional connection."

"We were connected."

"In bed."

"And out of it. We got along, Chloe. You complemented
my life. I made yours more interesting."

Perhaps he had known her better than she'd thought.
"And this time you're not offering marriage."

"Not at first, no." There was something in his expression she couldn't read, but she thought maybe she didn't need to.

"You don't trust me."

"Do you trust me?" he asked.

She thought about it. She hadn't...when she'd left him, she hadn't trusted him at all. Or she would have stayed to talk it out as he'd planned to do.

Did she trust him now? Two years on and hopefully wiser. "You're like my father in more ways than I thought in the beginning."

"But not his mirror image. I will be a true papa to my children. Not like my father, not like yours."

In this, Chloe believed Ariston completely. "You had one of the best role models."

"Pappous. Yes."

"I wonder how your father turned out the way he did?" she mused.

"Nature over nurture."

Chloe had to agree. Takis would never have *raised* his son to be so congenitally selfish. "Bad genes somewhere back in the family line."

"Everyone has them."

"No doubt."

"Will you risk it?"

Would she? Risk going after what she wanted when she knew heartbreak might well be at the end of her journey? "My sister?"

"I'll do my best by her. I'll even require couples counseling between her and her husband as part of the deal if that will make you feel better."

Chloe laughed, but nodded. "You know, I think it would. Neither of us grew up with a role model for what constitutes a good marriage."

"Then it will be done." He got up and walked purposefully to his briefcase.

He pulled out a pen and then grabbed the red bound document. Flipping it open, he leafed through the pages until he reached the one he was looking for. Then, he wrote something on a page about a quarter of the way in.

"You're really adding that?"

"Yes."

"I'll do it."

"To guarantee your sister gets marriage counseling?" Ariston asked with some amusement.

"To give her the best hope at happiness in her future. Sinking under the burden of Dioletis Industries isn't it."

"Tell her. Forty-eight hours." Ariston tossed the red folio back to Chloe.

She caught it. "What if Rhea wants clarification, or to negotiate?"

"It's completely unambiguous, but she can call if she has a question. As for negotiation, she's got nothing I want."

"You said you wanted me." After the mind-blowing sex they'd shared the night before, she knew that was still true.

"On *your* terms, not hers." He settled back onto the bed beside Chloe, his fingertip tracing the edge of the sheet covering her breasts. "If you have stipulations, I will listen to them."

She pushed his hand away, unable to think while he was doing that. "Are you going to keep Dioletis Industries as its own concern?"

It wasn't a stipulation. She was just curious. More so than she'd thought she'd be. Again she thought Ariston might know her better than she'd given him credit for, maybe even better than she knew herself in some instances.

"The company will retain its name, but will become a subsidiary of SSE. I will be requiring a much bigger block of shares this time around. Major restructuring will have to take place to make the company profitable again."

"Rhea said as much."

He nodded. "I can't guarantee all the employees will keep their current positions, but I will keep as many within Dioletis Industries as possible. Those that lose their places entirely will be put in my company's job reassignment program. Eighty percent of the employees placed in the program find new employment within Spiridakou and Sons Enterprises."

"Thank you."

He shrugged. "It is what you came to me for, isn't it? To keep people employed."

"Yes." But mostly for Rhea, though Chloe was aware that made her every bit as self-serving as the next person. "Will Rhea retain a position within the company?"

She couldn't make it a condition of the agreement, not with so many people's livelihoods, not to mention Rhea's own future, riding on Ariston's goodwill. However, Chloe couldn't help hoping he would show her sister more mercy than her own father had ever shown either of his daughters.

"She will be CEO, but the job will alter significantly with the takeover. She'll work with a team, her own duties more specific than they are now. Just like my other top management, she'll be required to take courses in not only team management strategy, but efficient delegation and work life effectiveness as well."

"That sounds amazing."

"I'm glad you think so. Ultimately, she will also answer to me, as all my other top management does. The survival of the company will no longer rest on her shoulders."

No, it would rest on Ariston's and Chloe had no doubts that not only could her tycoon husband handle the added pressure, he would guide Dioletis Industries into the modern global economy with great success.

"Thank you." It was far more than Chloe had expected.

He shrugged. "I prefer you content with our arrangement. It is give and take."

"But not with Rhea." Chloe indicated the proposal that he'd said was nonnegotiable.

"My policy has always been to limit my negotiations with principals only."

And despite the fact that Rhea was now the majority stock controller in Dioletis Industries, from Ariston's viewpoint she was not a principal.

As he'd said, *Rhea* had nothing he wanted.

He didn't consider Chloe an unwitting pawn to be used at his discretion. In that way, at least, Ariston was definitely not like her father.

"Takis always said you lived in a black-and-white world, while the rest of us existed with shades of gray," she said, rather than revealing any of her tumbling thoughts.

"Perhaps in some things. Others I am willing to compromise on. Like I would prefer to have you in my bed from tonight forward, but I will wait until your sister accepts the terms of my offer."

"I can't make a permanent move that quickly!" This impatience was one of the few things she hadn't missed about Ariston. "I've got a business."

"The small art supply store and gallery in Oregon."

She didn't take *small* to be a pejorative term. Her shop and gallery were literally small in both store size and business conducted. She could live off the proceeds, but nothing like as lavishly as she had done with him, or even growing up with her father. "Yes."

"You cannot run a business on the West Coast and be

my lover." There was no particular edge to his tone, but there was no give either.

"I know." Just as she couldn't be a student and his wife. "The gallery is just starting to thrive, though."

The art supply shop had been a success from the start. She'd done her homework and discovered that though there was a thriving artist community in the town she wanted to settle in, they had to drive nearly an hour for decent supplies. Now she drew both the amateur and professional artists from up and down the coast because she carried what they liked, what serious artists looked for in the way of charcoals, paints and other supplies.

She wasn't sure the fact her small gallery was paying its own mortgage and for a part-time employee would register with the billionaire businessman, though.

"I am aware. You should be proud of building such a sturdy concern." No surprise at her success or mockery tinged his voice.

She found herself smiling with pleasure at his approval. "Thank you. I don't want to lose it."

"I would not ask you to."

But he had. Well, as good as.

"I have found an artist with a business degree who will run it for you. Her husband was forced into early retirement and she is keen for the opportunity. The fact you have an apartment above the gallery is of particular note, as they are days from eviction."

He offered this with the attitude of a man who had done his best to stack the deck and was pleased with his own efforts.

She had to admit she was impressed.

Both by his acumen and his unshakable confidence.

The fact he'd found yet another screw to put to her conscience in the form of a couple facing homelessness was

barely a blip on her radar. Not in the face of the unavoid-
able truth that he had planned all of this on the assumption
that not only would she come to him, but that she would
accept his terms for the business rescue.

"You really are a master manipulator."

He seemed pleased by the questionable compliment.
"I prefer to think of myself as fully prepared for every
contingency."

"What would have happened to that couple if I had refused your terms?" she demanded, amusement warring
with sheer awe at his determination to get his way.

"We'll never have to know now."

"Tell me you would have helped them somehow."

"You are the bleeding heart, not me."

"No. No one would accuse you of having a bleeding
heart." But it would have helped hers if he'd admitted to
having one at all.

"So?"

Hadn't they covered everything? They'd be having sex
for the foreseeable future, without birth control, in the
hopes of her getting pregnant.

And he would save hundreds of jobs and thereby the
people connected to them as well as Rhea's marriage.
"What?"

"Will you join me for dinner this evening?"

She discovered she wanted to say yes, but knew she
couldn't.

"I've got a flight home this afternoon." And now, more
than ever, she needed to keep it. "If I'm going to move to
New York to become your lover for the next three years,
there's a lot I've got to get put in order."

Not least of which was preparing to train the couple he'd
found to take over her gallery and store. Perhaps Chloe

should have been more upset at his high-handedness, but her predominant emotion was relief.

Relief that the store would be there for her if she needed it, and she hadn't had to figure out how to make that happen on her own. She didn't think she had it in her for a more dramatic reaction. Over the past twenty-four hours, her emotions had been wrung out and pegged up to dry.

"You have two weeks."

The ease of his capitulation shocked her. Nevertheless, she shook her head, trying for more time. "I'll need at least a month."

"The movers will be there to pack your things for delivery to your apartment in upper Manhattan tomorrow."

No wonder he hadn't pushed about her flying home. He'd already arranged movers.

He'd had no doubts at all that she would agree to his plan.

"I'm to have my own apartment?" Which, admittedly, was nearer his offices than the home they'd shared during their marriage, but she had not considered that sharing his bed did not equate to sharing his life.

"You're no longer my wife."

Right. Of course she wouldn't live with him.

There could be benefits to this arrangement, though. "I won't have to attend all the boring business dinners," she said with some satisfaction.

His lips twitched, but it wasn't in amusement—more like annoyance. "You never complained about them before."

"As you said, I was your wife then. I'm not now."

"Is that why you did not want our marriage to be permanent? Because you didn't like the social obligations that came with being a billionaire's wife?"

"I never said I didn't want our marriage to last."

"Your actions spoke for you."

"What actions?" Not only had she never complained about the aspects of her life as his wife she found onerous, she'd never once shirked them either.

"You were on birth control from the beginning."

"I had my reasons."

"Yes, you didn't feel obligated to keep your end of the bargain."

"Are you insane? I gave up my education, my dreams and the life I knew to follow through on that unholy contract between you and my father."

"And that contract stipulated a child."

"It stipulated what was to happen if there was a child, not that one should exist."

"The expectation was implied." He shifted on the bed, as if he wanted to move away, but he stayed where he was.

"But not spelled out."

"Is that how you plan to explain it to my grandfather?"

"Why should I explain it to him?"

"He's the reason I made that bargain with your father. My grandfather wanted great-grandchildren."

"And you set about getting them for him in the only way you knew how. Through a business deal."

"It was the most honest way, at least on my part."

Wow. He did sanctimonious almost as well as arrogance. "I wasn't dishonest with you. I never said I wouldn't use birth control."

"You never said you would either."

"You never asked."

"The contract implied—"

"Right, like you'd allow any supposed implication in a contract dictate your actions in business. You'd do what was best for you and your company and you know it."

"You are saying you believe not getting pregnant with my child was best for you?" Something moved in the depths of his eyes, but he wasn't letting it surface enough for her to read what it meant.

"I was twenty, gaga over a man who considered me part of a business deal and resentful of my father's manipulations and the sacrifices I'd been forced to make for a company that had brought nothing but grief to me and my mother before me."

"You are in much the same situation now. Why agree to these terms yet again?"

Again, wow. He hadn't even reacted to her admission that she'd been crazy about him and had as good as implied he knew she still was.

She tugged the sheet higher and looked past him, toward the bedspread piled on the floor, left there the night before when they'd been frantic to get to the bed. "They aren't the exact same terms, though, are they?"

"You will not use birth control this time."

"I said I wouldn't." That wasn't the only thing different, but he didn't need her pointing out the nuances of his proposition.

"Because it was spelled out as part of the deal," he mocked.

"Precisely." And he wasn't going to make her feel bad about her past choices.

She had enough of her own regrets on that count.

"And you will not attend *boring* business dinners with me."

"I might…if you ask nicely."

"You *have* changed."

"Having your heart broken will do that to a person."

"Who broke your heart?" he asked in a dangerous tone.

"Who do you think?" He really had no clue how much she'd loved him.

Because to him, she had been nothing more than part

of a business deal. She still was, only one he'd spelled out more precisely.

Something she'd do herself no favors forgetting.

"Are you trying to imply it was me?" he asked with a full measure of disbelief.

"My father had his own fair share of the responsibility in that regard, but yes, you."

"How did I break your heart?"

"Losing you hurt. A lot."

"But you walked out."

Because she'd felt she had no choice. "Because you saw me as nothing more than a business asset."

"No, I did not. However our marriage came into being, it was a marriage. I treated you with respect and consideration as my wife." His tone dared her to deny it.

She couldn't and didn't want to. If his words hadn't been true, she wouldn't be agreeing to this new deal, not even for the sake of the sister she loved so much and hundreds of faceless employees that relied on her family's company for their livelihood.

He brushed his fingers along the edge of the sheet again, heat filling his azure gaze. "I do not think you can blame me for your broken heart."

He was right. She was the one who'd walked out. She just hadn't realized how much it would hurt to do so—and to stay away, or how much she'd been hoping he'd come after her. He finally had, but not in a way she could have expected.

Though she probably should have.

Ariston was no knight in shining armor, seeking the heart of a fair damsel. He was a pragmatic tycoon with his own agenda and unique sense of honor.

"So, the movers are coming tomorrow," she commented,

rather than continuing a discussion that would only lead to revelations she had no desire to make.

"Yes."

"But you said I had two weeks." And she'd asked for more and he'd just ignored her.

"I'm afraid you'll have to live out of a suitcase at the local hotel in the interim."

Amazing. He was beyond self-assured. He was scarily confident of getting his own way, but then wasn't she letting him have it?

"How did you know I would come to you?" Much less that she would agree to his deal.

"You made the appointment with my secretary last week."

"But still…you made all these plans in a week?"

"Does it matter?"

"Yes."

"Let me rephrase. It does not matter."

"Seriously?" It was all she could do not to roll her eyes at him like a teenager, but really, did he have to try so hard to bring that out in her? "You haven't gotten any less arrogant in two years."

"Why should I?"

"Life usually handles that for most people."

"My life has shown me that I must make the things happen that are necessary."

"Mine has shown me that no matter how much I want some things, no matter how hard I work, I'll never have them."

"What has left you so disappointed?" He asked as if the answer really mattered to him, when she knew it couldn't.

"You wouldn't understand." He really, really wouldn't. And with that, she realized it was time for her to escape. She pushed at his hip and chest. "I need a shower."

"You have time."

"Weren't you on your way out the door?"

"Perhaps I will put off my first meeting of the day."

"No." She practically yelled her denial. "My plane—"

"Leaves in a few hours, I know. And you'll want to give your sister the news." His eyes traveled over Chloe's curves under the thin sheet, saying without words what he'd rather she spend her time doing.

"You know too much," she grumbled.

"There was a time when I didn't, to my own detriment."

"I can't imagine it."

"Neither could I, but it did happen."

"When?"

"You need to ask?"

She blinked. "Yes." Did he think she was a mind reader?

"The birth control."

"But you did know about it."

"Not until shortly before we left New York for our final trip together to Athens."

"By then, I'd stopped taking it," she shared with gallows irony she wasn't sure he'd get.

"What?" For the first time in their acquaintance, her ex-husband, the mighty Ariston Spiridakou looked 100 percent gobsmacked. "But then you could have been..."

"Pregnant when I left you? Yes, for a month I was very much afraid I was."

A month during which she'd been terrified she'd allowed herself to become pregnant only to discover that the man she loved and had called husband felt nothing for her. She could have waited to make sure, but she'd known if she didn't leave while he was out of country, the chances of her doing so at all dropped dramatically.

When she'd discovered she wasn't pregnant, she'd been in equal parts relieved and devastated.

No excuse to go back to him, no stay in her bid for building a new life without him. It was about that time she'd stopped eating and a couple of months later that Rhea had staged her intervention, encouraging Chloe to return to the West Coast, where she'd gone to art school and fallen in love with a different type of life.

"But you were not?" His face leached of color and the hands on either side of her hips fisted in tension.

"Do you really need to ask?"

"You could have…"

"No, *I* could not. You really can be an idiot, Ariston." With that she shoved him out of the way and jumped from the bed, uncaring of her nudity, as done with their conversation as she had ever been.

The great big stupid idiot.

# CHAPTER SEVEN

ARISTON watched his ex-wife storm into the en suite with a sense of utter shock coursing through him.

She'd stopped taking the pill about the same time he'd discovered she'd been using it. What terrible timing.

She had intended to fulfill her part of their marriage contract—she'd just clearly had her own timeframe for doing so. As he was famous for telling his CEOs, a bit of communication would have helped.

And she was angry with him?

He shook his head, not for the first time, at the vagaries of the female psyche and his ex-wife's in particular.

She could have been pregnant when she left. That infuriated him, but it also confused him. Why leave before she knew whether or not she was? Why stop taking birth control, thereby showing intention to make their marriage long-term only to end up leaving after all?

For the first time in his life, Ariston had absolutely no clue to the puzzle before him and he found that more than a bit frustrating.

Had she felt too young for motherhood? While she hadn't said as much, Chloe had revealed a level of bitterness at her circumstances he would never have guessed at. Feelings she'd apparently needed to work through before being willing to have his baby.

One thing was certain, her coming off the pill—even in the eleventh hour of their marriage—blew his initial assessment of what she'd wanted out of their marriage all to hell.

Though he was a man who hated to be wrong, he found he didn't mind in this instance.

And regardless of the past, soon she would be exactly where he wanted her, back in his bed on a permanent basis.

Unlike what Chloe had implied with her question about his lovers during their two years apart, he'd hardly had legions of sexual partners since she'd left Greece. The few he'd taken to bed since the divorce had only proven one thing to him. Once a supremely congenial lover was found, no one else measured up.

While he did not believe in romantic drivel like all-consuming love, he did believe in sexual compatibility. And he and Chloe had that in spades.

Against all of Ariston's expectations, when he'd married the artsy, somewhat introverted and extremely innocent daughter of his business associate, Chloe had turned out to be the most amazing lover he'd ever had.

She didn't play sexual power games, but gave him everything in her responses, holding nothing back. Her honest, awakening passions had become addictive in a way Ariston had neither expected nor been happy about once he learned of her subterfuge about the birth control.

But he had no intention of ever admitting it to anyone, and Chloe least of all—she'd been gone from his bed only two years, but that had been one year, eleven months and twenty-nine days too long.

He didn't like feeling weak, and needing her sexually had done that to him.

Eventually, he'd realized that the problem wasn't how much he'd enjoyed bedding his ex-wife, it was that he'd allowed the balance of power to shift in their relationship in a way he never would have done in any other business deal.

This new deal was much more weighted in his favor. And that was just the way he intended to keep it. No matter what revelations she made about the past.

It had taken him only six months to realize he wanted his wife back, but another eighteen to bring everything into place so that it could happen—on his terms.

She would make an ideal mother. He'd thought so from the beginning. So had his grandfather.

Ariston might give the appearance of an American businessman and speak English without an accent, but at heart Ariston Spiridakou was a Greek man.

Despite his own parents doing their best to destroy it, he still had a strong sense of family and heritage. He wanted offspring, children that would never be neglected as he had been.

He'd expected Chloe to provide the other half of that equation. And with her purely Greek lineage, even though she'd been raised entirely in the United States, she'd found favor with his grandfather as well.

Once she'd met him, she'd charmed Pappous as well, cementing her role in their family, though Ariston hadn't realized how permanent that was until he'd filed for divorce.

Pappous had been apoplectic.

Unused to upsetting the one person in the world Ariston did not want to disappoint, he'd been more than a little dismayed by his grandfather's reaction to losing Chloe from their small family.

Even after Ariston told the old man she'd been on birth control, he'd ranted at Ariston, being the one to first suggest maybe she'd been too young to face motherhood yet.

An old-fashioned man, Takis Spiridakou had still been furious when he learned Chloe hadn't been allowed to finish her university degree. Ariston doubted she had any idea what an ally she had in the strong-minded old Greek.

One thing both Ariston and Takis agreed on—Chloe was nothing like Ariston's own mother.

He hadn't been surprised at all that Chloe categorically refused to give him a child and walk away. She was not the type of woman to abandon her baby to be raised by others. Not that that had ever been Ariston's intention.

She'd shown herself to be tenderhearted and generous; he imagined that under the right circumstances, she would be willing to surrogate a child for someone else. But these weren't them.

And between the two of them, he was fairly certain, never could be. He didn't mind. He didn't want a mother for his children that saw them as a bargaining chip to ensure a certain lifestyle as he'd been for the woman who gave him birth.

But no matter how Chloe attempted to paint the past in a new light, one in which she was not obliged to fulfill the unwritten expectations of their contract, she'd hidden the fact she was on birth control from him.

He would have understood a desire to wait a year, or two. He would have changed the original terms of the contract to five years, in that case.

He wouldn't have liked it, but Ariston was a reasonable man. He would have done it.

But she hadn't given him the chance.

She'd simply deceived him.

For three years. Well, *almost* three years. He'd been no more aware she'd gone off the pill than that she'd been on it in the first place.

Ariston didn't like feeling ignorant any more than he did feeling weak. Even less so, if that were possible. Weakness he could control with his formidable will, but ignorance born of another's deception?

That was something he couldn't control and a complete anathema to him. And something he would make damn sure did not happen this time around with Chloe.

Regardless of recent revelations, he wasn't going to make the mistake of blindly trusting her innocence again.

Chloe was busy supervising movers and quietly plotting the most effective way to murder her ex-husband for his impatience when her phone rang for the umpteenth time in an hour. She sent it to voice mail without even looking at who the caller was.

Avoiding the curious looks of the movers, Chloe sighed and rubbed her forehead.

The man simply wasn't content to let her get on with putting things in order—he kept calling her.

First to tell her about the terms of the takeover. As if she cared. Bottom line? People kept their jobs and Rhea and Samuel's marriage had a chance of surviving.

Samuel had called to thank her and Chloe had gotten off the phone and cried at how happy and hopeful her sister's husband had sounded. Rhea had expressed her gratitude with heartfelt effusiveness when Chloe had dropped off Ariston's deal proposal with her.

Her sister was happy and that made Chloe happy.

But Ariston had wanted to tell her all the nitty-gritty details of a merger that Chloe had zero real interest in.

As if her sister hadn't kept Chloe on the phone for three hours the night before doing the same thing. Rhea had been ecstatic about some of the terms, but a little hurt about the marriage counseling requirement.

Samuel, on the other hand, had made it clear that was his favorite element to the proposal.

Chloe just wanted to forget about Dioletis Industries for the next few days while she got her own chaotic life in order.

She had had plenty to think about already. Plenty to keep her tossing and turning and sleepless for most of the night.

She'd still been zombielike and on her second cup of coffee when the movers arrived this morning.

Organizing her move was hard enough in her exhausted condition without Ariston's constant phone calls.

Less than an hour after the one about the contract, he'd called to tell her about the apartment she'd be living in, after texting her enough pictures to fill up her text in-box storage.

The apartment was beautiful and bigger than what she was living in now, but really? She'd see it when she got there. Right?

And right now, she couldn't care less about its original moldings and hardwood floors throughout. The urge to run away that she'd had in his office was back in full force.

No matter how much she wanted to be with Ariston, Chloe wasn't so naive that she didn't realize the risk to her heart was huge.

The call asking her which designer she currently favored had technically come from Jean, who wanted to set up appointments at several of New York's boutiques.

But the source of the call had been Ariston.

Chloe was feeling pressed enough trying to button down her life in two weeks—she didn't need the extra pressure of scheduling her new life in New York already on top of it.

He'd called at lunch time to make sure she was taking a break to eat. Seriously?

Ariston was the least likely candidate for that kind of solicitude she could imagine.

When she'd said something to that effect, he'd taken her crankiness as a sign she *hadn't* eaten. He'd been right.

Arrogant, pushy tycoon.

The phone rang again and she went to press the forward-to-voicemail key, only to realize that it wasn't her phone ringing. It was one of the movers'. That was it. She was definitely changing her ringtone to something more personal. Just as soon as she could get someone else to do it for her.

Technology wasn't exactly her friend.

The mover who had answered his phone had a strange expression on his face and he was walking toward her.

"It's…uh…Mr. Spiridakou. He…uh…wanted to talk to you." The mover put the phone out toward her.

She groaned and rolled her eyes, not caring who saw her reaction, but she took the phone. "Yes, Ariston?"

"I believe your phone is broken. I've instructed Jean to get you a new one immediately."

"It's not broken. I forwarded your call to voice mail."

"My last *three* calls?"

"Are you sure there were three?" She thought about it and conceded maybe he was right. She sighed. "Yes, *three* of them."

"But why?"

"Ariston, you can't call me every ten minutes while I'm trying to oversee the packing up of my apartment." She couldn't help the exasperation-borderline-irritation in her tone.

"Surely they are done by now. Your current accommodations are not precisely capacious."

She couldn't deny the one-bedroom apartment above

her gallery was small, but it was hers. And she wasn't exactly relishing leaving it.

Even to be with Ariston.

"I'm sorting as we go." And if she was taking her time doing so, that was her business.

"You can sort when you arrive in New York."

"I doubt it." As if he was going to give her the time. "I remember how hectic my life was with you before."

"You will not have the responsibilities you once did. You will not be my wife."

"I know that, but you've already had Jean calling me to set up shopping appointments, for goodness' sake."

"You'll need new clothes."

"Right, because my old clothes from the city are so worn." They might not be this year's collections, but she favored the designers she did because of their classic lines and minimal use of ephemeral trends.

"They are out-of-date, surely. It's been two years."

"Ariston, I'm not particularly fussed if they are a couple of seasons out-of-date."

"Besides, you have lost weight. You will need a smaller size. For now, anyway."

Well, *that* explained his call about lunch. He thought she was too thin. He wasn't alone. Her doctor had been hounding her to put on a minimum of ten pounds, but Chloe hadn't taken the need to do so seriously.

She wasn't dangerously underweight. Just maybe headed in that direction. "I'm fine. My clothes are fine."

"Why wouldn't you want new clothes?" he asked, sounding bewildered.

"It's not that."

"Then?"

"Fine…I'll buy new clothes. Just let me get back to packing."

"You mean sorting."

"Yes."

His snort said what he thought of her insistence on doing it now. "I called because I wanted to know if you would prefer a different apartment. You didn't seem all that excited about the one I sent you pictures of."

"It's beautiful. Why would you say that? I told you I liked it. A lot."

"But you do not love it."

"It's just an apartment, Ariston."

"It is where you will be living, for the foreseeable future."

"I am aware."

"So?"

"I'm sure it will be just fine."

"I do not strive for fine."

No, he didn't. She'd always known he was an overachiever. She'd never believed he had even the narrowest of streaks of insecurity, though. "It's more than fine. It's wonderful. Really."

"If you're sure."

"Yes, now I've got to go." She tried to keep her tone patient. "I'm sure you have more important things to attend to."

"I was in a meeting," he admitted in a strange tone.

She didn't know how to respond to that. She couldn't picture the man she'd been married to ducking out of a meeting to call and make sure she was happy with the apartment he'd chosen for his...well, not *mistress,* but she wouldn't call herself his lover either.

Not when he would not, or simply could not, love her.

"If you are sure the apartment is to your liking."

"It is, very much," she added, not wanting a repeat of this phone call.

"I will talk to you later."

"Sure. Talk to you tomorrow," she hinted.

The call ended from his end and she figured he'd gone back to his meeting.

When her phone buzzed in her pocket an hour later, she knew better than to forward it to voice mail.

She grabbed it and pressed the connect button with more force than necessary. "Look, if you're still worried about the apartment, don't be. I said it was fine," she said, thoroughly frustrated. "I had no idea you could be so insecure."

"Hello, Chloe."

It was a male voice, but it wasn't Ariston's.

A sick feeling settled in the pit of her stomach. "Father."

"I called to thank you for saving the company. It means a great deal to me."

"I didn't do it for you."

Silence met that pronouncement.

"I did it for Rhea and the hundreds of employees your mismanagement would have put out of work."

"I did not call to be insulted."

That was a given.

"Why *did* you call?"

"To say thank you, as I have done."

"Though you had nothing to do with my motives, I acknowledge your appreciation. I guess we're done, then?" she said hopefully, wanting nothing more than to get off the phone with this man who had spent a lot more years hurting her far more than her ex-husband ever had.

"You're never going to forgive me, are you? Even though he's taking you back."

"I walked out. Not him."

"But he'd drawn up the divorce papers."

She didn't need that reminder. "We aren't getting married again anyway."

"I heard."

"Oh?"

"I spoke to Rhea." If he expected her to feel guilty for not calling in two years, he was bound to be disappointed.

"I'm sorry. I could have negotiated a better deal for both of my daughters if you'd come to me instead of Ariston first."

Oh, no, he was not going there. "Even retired and facing the collapse of your company, you're as arrogant and business-minded as ever. I don't need you negotiating *anything* for me. No matter how you see the situation between us, it was your treating me like an asset to bargain with in the first place that was the problem."

"I was looking toward your future." His voice was almost pleading.

"The company's future you mean."

"It is one and the same."

"No, it is not. Not for me and not for Rhea. She almost lost her marriage because of that stupid company."

"It wouldn't have been a great loss. Samuel brought nothing to their union."

"He brought himself and that's all that Rhea needed, but you couldn't let them be happy."

"Their marital problems are not my fault."

"Aren't they? You're the one that insisted Rhea had to take over Dioletis Industries, even though you knew she and Samuel had agreed to have children."

"Now you're blaming me for her miscarriages?"

"The doctor said her job was too high-stress."

"She's the CEO of a major concern—of course the job is high-stress."

"You stepped down for your health, but expected her to

compromise hers and that of her unborn children for the good of the company."

"Rhea is only twenty-nine. She has plenty of time for motherhood if indeed she really wants it."

"Oh, she does. And she'll have it, along with a strong marriage, if I have anything to say about it."

"She understands her duty."

"Like you understood yours?"

"Yes."

"You were clueless about your duty to our family, but Rhea is not going to be like that."

"She told me about the marriage counseling." The derision Chloe expected was missing from her father's tone. "Perhaps your mother and I would have been happier if we had done something like that."

Chloe didn't know what to say. "That was unexpected."

"I loved your mother, Chloe. I love my daughters."

"You've got a lousy way of showing it."

"I'm learning that."

Wow. This was so not like the father she remembered. "Who's been talking to you?" she wondered.

"Believe it or not, Samuel."

"Seriously?"

"He is a social worker. It's his job to have insights like that."

"He's very good at his job."

"I'm sure you're right."

"I'm glad to hear you say that."

"I'm sorry about Rhea's miscarriages," her father said in a tone that cracked with emotion.

"You said—"

"I know. Admitting when I am wrong is not my strong suit."

"No."

"I may have been wrong five years ago, but please believe I had your future in mind as much as the company's."

"I'm not sure I can."

He sighed. "I want you to be happy, Chloe. I want that for Rhea as well. This deal with Ariston, I think it will make that possible, but I don't want to see you hurt again."

"Perhaps you should have thought of that before planning yet another business marriage before my first one was over."

"Yes, I should have."

"You mean that?" she asked with more hope than she'd thought she had left where her remaining parent was concerned.

"I do and I'm sorry."

She'd never heard her father apologize. Not once. Not ever. She took a deep breath, feeling the sting of tears in the back of her eyes. "I forgive you."

"Thank you. That means more than I can say."

"How's your blood pressure?" she asked without planning to.

"Much better. I'm exercising, eating right...but I miss my old life."

"As chairman of Dioletis Industries."

"As father to my children."

"Rhea still sees you."

"A lot less frequently than you might imagine. She never forgave me for how hurt you were by your marriage to Ariston."

Chloe hadn't known that. "She never said anything to me."

"She said plenty to me," her father said ruefully.

"The company will retain its name, but it's going to be absorbed by SSE," Chloe felt the need to say.

"I know and in a way, I'm very relieved. It cost me my

wife, it cost me my daughters and eventually it cost my health."

"But you still love it."

"Yes."

Finally there was something she and her father had in common. Loving unwisely. "It will be okay. Maybe grandchildren will make up for retirement."

"I'm hoping you and Rhea will allow me the privilege of that role, though I'm fully aware I don't deserve it."

Wow. This humble side to her father was not something she was used to dealing with. "Just don't try to turn them into little CEOs."

"I'll leave that to Ariston."

"He'll have to deal with me."

"A formidable concept, I am sure."

Chloe found herself laughing with her father for the first time in years. "Yes, it is."

"Thank you, Chloe."

"You're welcome."

"I love you." It was the first time he'd said it since she was eleven years old.

The tears threatening finally spilled and Chloe didn't try to hide them from her voice when she said, "I love you too."

"Please don't cut me out of your life again."

"Don't be an arrogant, cold manipulator, and I won't."

He laughed alone this time, but she was smiling.

"I won't," he promised.

And she thought maybe this time, it was a promise her father intended to keep.

# CHAPTER EIGHT

IT took Chloe closer to three weeks than two to train her replacements and put her affairs in order.

Though she'd only lived in the small coastal community that catered to tourists for less than two years, she'd built up a life there. One that wasn't defined entirely by the time she spent in her gallery and shop.

She was an adjunct member of the chamber of commerce as well as fundraising coordinator for their annual dinner auction. Finding someone to fulfill her community responsibilities took all her time outside her hours in the shop.

Well, the hours not taken up by Ariston's frequent phone calls. He hadn't been happy when she'd changed her flight to a week later before telling him.

He'd been positively cranky when she'd started making noises about having to do so again. That conversation had happened the night before and she hadn't heard from him since. She would be grateful if she wasn't certain it was the calm before the storm.

She might even miss the calls, though she wouldn't admit that—even under pressure.

While she was concerned about a lot of things, she wasn't worried he'd changed his mind. According to Rhea the merger/takeover was in full swing.

Chloe's musings were interrupted by the soft chimes announcing a customer in the gallery. Her new managers were organizing an inventory delivery in the shop next door, so she was manning the gallery alone. One of her final opportunities to do so—she was relishing her time here.

It had been a quiet morning, however, since they'd opened an hour ago.

Looking forward to interacting with a customer, she got up from her desk. She'd been making a list of people to contact in hopes of finding a new fundraising coordinator to replace her. So far, there were only two names on it and neither was she keen on.

The one woman she'd thought *would* do a stellar job had turned Chloe down because of prior commitments.

Forcing away the discouraging thoughts, Chloe curved her lips in her routine customer-welcoming smile only to have it freeze as she recognized her visitor.

"Ariston! What are you doing here?"

"Collecting my errant lover." His cerulean gaze was too serious to be kidding.

"But—"

"I have brought a professional fundraiser and event planner with me," he said, interrupting whatever she'd been about to say.

And honestly, Chloe wasn't sure what that was. In order to have arrived right now, he'd have had to have left New York at the crack of dawn to have made the cross-continental flight, not to mention the drive from the nearest airport that could service his company jet.

Chloe's gaze slid to the polished woman standing at Ariston's side. Wearing a suit by a midlevel designer that would impress, but not intimidate the locals, the woman's smile was just as perfectly targeted.

She put her manicured hand out. "Angela Carston. It's a pleasure to meet you, Mrs. Spiridakou."

"Ms., actually." Chloe shook the other woman's hand. "But you can call me Chloe. You're really here for the annual dinner auction?"

"Angela, please. And your husband is paying me a very nice fee to do just that, yes."

"Ex...*husband,* that is. And thank you for being here, regardless of your reasons for doing it. I'll be able to fly to New York once I get you up to speed on what's been done so far and our objectives for the auction."

She turned to Ariston, but he looked a lot less pleased than she would have expected now that he was irrefutably getting his way.

"That should only take me a few hours, at most," she told him. "This isn't a Spiridakou & Sons Enterprises event, or even close to that magnitude."

He didn't smile, but he did nod. "Good. You can do so on the plane back to New York."

"She can't do the job from New York."

"She will not. Angela will fly back commercially later this week."

"Why did you make her fly out to begin with, then?" She frowned at him, not liking the idea the other woman had been forced duplicate travel on Chloe's behalf. "You could have told me about it over the phone."

"I assumed you would want to meet Angela before you allowed her to take over."

"You didn't show me the same courtesy regarding my own business." Though she had to give him full marks for his choice in managers for her store and gallery.

The middle-aged couple were both enamored of the art world and Chloe had liked the wife's work so much, she'd offered a permanent revolving spot in her gallery for the woman to sell her pottery.

"They were ideal," he countered, as if reading her mind.

She smiled, unable to help herself. "They are."

"And yet you are not in New York today." His frown held something akin to consternation.

"I'm not leaving here without making sure my obligations are all taken care of."

"So you said on the phone last night."

"And your answer was to hire a fundraising expert?"

His shrug said it all.

If he saw a problem, he fixed it.

Chloe shook her head. "You're probably paying Angela more than the funds we expect to raise with the auction."

"I offered to donate a lump sum in lieu of the auction." There was no mistaking the disgruntlement he felt at her rejection of his money.

"The auction isn't just about raising funds for community projects. It's a social event residents of the area look forward to all year long."

"That was the impression you gave, yes."

"Ariston!"

"What?"

"You're very frustrating."

"I do not understand why. You expressed your concerns and here am I, meeting them."

Suddenly realizing that she and Ariston had stood there talking as if Angela wasn't even in the gallery, Chloe felt heat crawl up her cheeks. She had ignored the other woman's presence to the extent that Chloe had as good as gotten into an argument with Ariston in front of her.

A headache forming right behind her left eye, Chloe turned to the newly hired event coordinator and grimaced apologetically. "Please pardon my lack of manners. Thank you very much for flying across country at a moment's notice to take on this job."

"I'm happy to be here," Angela replied, looking supremely unfazed by her very last-minute double cross-continental trips.

"Not that you'll be here very long at this point." Chloe's grimace slipped into a full frown. "You can't be looking forward to hopping right back onto the plane."

Angela smiled winningly. "My job often calls for travel and I've got to say, flying in the Spiridakou jet is a lot more comfortable than commercial."

"It is," Chloe had to agree. "But even the most comfortable transportation doesn't make up for spending so many hours of a single day in the air."

"I notice you evince no concern on my behalf," Ariston interjected in a teasing tone.

She found no humor to match his at that moment. "You do exactly what you like, Ariston."

"Are you implying that I shanghaied Angela? I can assure you that is not the case."

"No, indeed," the event coordinator affirmed. "Ariston presented a very appealing offer, both in terms of remuneration and scope."

"Then, here's hoping his perception meets reality for you." Because Chloe would not be happy with either of them if Angela didn't follow through on the job.

If Chloe put their departure off with one more excuse, Ariston fully intended to simply pick her up and carry her off to the airport.

She'd insisted she needed to go over things with her new managers one last time, and then that the mayor had to meet Angela Carston and approve her taking over Chloe's role as fundraiser for the community auction. Chloe hadn't stopped there though, as Ariston might reasonably expect.

No, she'd then been adamant that she needed to call one of the local artists personally and tell him she was leaving for New York. According to Chloe, she'd already introduced him to the new managers, but the artist was both brilliant and a recluse, which meant a little extra coddling to make sure he knew he wasn't being forgotten.

Ariston had actually found himself getting jealous until Chloe informed him the artist was in his sixties and determinedly gay.

When she'd said…finally…that she needed to pack her things up in the hotel room, that at least Ariston had been able to do something about. He'd instructed his security team to take care of it while Chloe and Angela met with the mayor.

But the meeting was over and Ariston was ready to be on the road. Had been hours ago, to be precise. "Come, Chloe. It is a ninety-minute drive to the airport."

"Yes, I know." Chloe took a last sweeping glance around her hotel room, much as she had the gallery when they'd left it.

He did not see what could have put that wistful look in her emerald eyes. "Surely you will not miss living out of suitcases?"

"I wasn't," she contradicted while following him to the car.

"No. You had unpacked and organized your belongings as if preparing for a long stay." He helped her into the back of the rented limo and the door shut behind them.

"Where is Angela?"

"She's riding with the security team in the SUV."

Chloe craned her neck to see out the tinted windows. "But I thought we were going to discuss what she will be doing in my stead."

"Didn't you already cover it in your meeting with the mayor?" he asked with some exasperation.

"Not all of it."

"You will have plenty of time on the plane."

The limo started to move and Chloe finally nodded and settled back in her seat.

They rode in silence for several miles, leaving the small town behind. Chloe's beautiful green eyes never once strayed from the view out the window.

"You will miss your life here," he realized aloud.

"Yes."

Her easy agreement with no caveat that she was looking forward to returning to their life together bothered him. Her life here had been short and not where she was supposed to be.

He felt compelled to ask, "Do you regret agreeing to my proposal?"

"Business proposition, you mean," she said very carefully, her tone tired and tinged with sadness he did not like to hear.

No more did he understand it. He was offering her a life only a minuscule number would ever witness, much less truly experience.

"You will never want for anything," he promised her. "You will not regret returning to the Spiridakou family."

"Won't I?" Her troubled green gaze remained fixed on the view out the window.

A sense of impending doom had him crossing the limo, reaching to close the privacy window between the driver and them as he sat down beside her. "No, you will not. This is my vow to you."

Finally, she looked up at him, emerald gaze measuring. "It isn't something you can control, Ariston."

"We shall see." He would not argue with her. He would show her.

Then she would believe him and he would not even say, *I told you so.* In the interim, the time had come to remind her one of the reasons they worked as a couple.

Cupping her cheek, the feel of her soft skin under his hand hitting him deep in his gut, he lowered his head toward hers.

"What are you doing?" she gasped.

He smiled, letting his lips brush hers. "If you have forgotten, then three weeks is definitely too long to be apart."

Her eyes widened, but her mouth parted, inviting his kiss.

He lost no time accepting the sweet invitation, claiming her mouth with intent. This woman was his and the sooner she realized her life here in Oregon had only been a blip in their life together, the better. By her own admission, she had not wanted their marriage to end.

The time had come for her to remember why.

He took his time relearning her lips after their three weeks apart, tracing their lush bow shape with his tongue.

She made the soft whimpering sound he'd come to know intimately during their marriage, but this time it was laced with a desperation he would never have guessed at as she melted into him. No matter how she said she would miss her life here, she had missed him more.

He mapped her body through the oversized silk top she wore with leggings that disguised her weight loss to the eye. But his touch revealed how much closer to the surface her ribcage was.

He had already hired a personal trainer who would help Chloe gain necessary pounds while strengthening her muscles and preparing her body for the ordeal of pregnancy. No way was he going to allow her to risk herself carrying his child.

Her breasts were smaller than they had been, barely a handful and he did not care. Just touching her already pebble-hard nipples through the double layer of thin silk of her top and bra turned him on to the point of pain.

His sex strained against its confinement, the need to be inside her growing to near unbearable proportions.

He pulled her onto his lap, guiding her to straddle him so the apex of her thighs rubbed against his straining erection, despite their clothing. Pleasure erupted from him in a loud groan and he dove under her blouse to undo the catch on her bra.

It was a frontal closure and he smiled with satisfaction against her lips as he revealed her small but enticing curves to his questing fingers.

Sounds of pleasure and need fell from her lips to his as she rocked against him, clearly enjoying their position as much as he did.

He went to pull her top off and suddenly she went rigid above him, tearing her mouth from his. "You can't do that. Not here."

He laughed, the sound edged by the pain of his arousal. "I assure you, I can. We can."

"We're in the back of a car," she said, her face and tone twisted with horror.

"It is a limo and this would not be the first time we made love in the back of one." Though it had only happened once before, when they were on the long drive to her father's weekend home in upstate New York.

"That was different."

"How? These windows are tinted, as are those on the Spiridakou fleet of limousines. I have closed the privacy panel. We have an hour-plus drive before we reach the airport." He had not stopped touching her the entire time he was talking, squeezing and abrading her nipples until they grew hot against his fingertips.

She was so damn sexy, her innocent nature only making her more so.

"You're not playing fair," she accused.

"I am not playing at all." Recapturing her lips, he showed her just how far from a game he found the sex between them.

He went carnal with the kiss, doing what he knew would push her to the brink of the insanity of pleasure...and beyond.

This time, when he went to remove her clothes, she helped him, squirming out of her leggings while frantically trying to unbutton his shirt.

He'd discarded his suit jacket upon entering the limo, but though he'd loosened his tie, he still wore it. She didn't seem to care, her fingers scrabbling with buttons and then running over his chest as she panted against his lips.

He would have laughed, but didn't have the breath as he tore off the shirt and tie, shoving his slacks and boxers down his thighs and kicking them off.

Only then did he remember that he'd forgotten something he needed in the pocket. She made a mewling protest as he lifted her off his lap and placed her on the seat beside him. "What?" she asked wildly, her lovely oval face flushed with desire, her pupils so dilated her green eyes almost looked black.

"Condom."

# CHAPTER NINE

CHLOE'S brows drew together. "Isn't that the point? No birth control."

"Not until you have put on a few necessary pounds."

"What?" she asked, her tone filled with confusion. "Why?"

"You are dangerously thin."

"I am not."

"I have spoken to your doctor."

"You shouldn't have done. You had no right."

"You never rescinded the medical power of attorney you signed during our marriage." Though spouses had such rights automatically in many countries, their very global lifestyle required all contingencies had been planned for.

"You signed one too. How would you like me to make an invasive call to Dr. Helios?"

"I rescinded that power of attorney when our divorce became final."

She made a defensive move to cover herself and he swore. Damn it. He had not intended to take her out of the moment.

He grabbed the condom and put it on the seat beside him before reaching for her.

Running his hands over her silky skin, he had to swallow against his suddenly dry throat. "Listen to me, *yineka mou,* you must not let memories of the past intrude on our present. We have moved beyond them."

"You're so sure."

In this instance, he had more hope than certainty, but he would not admit it. She would be his. The change in plans he'd made before leaving New York seemed even more necessary now.

"We have both learned from our past, I hope." He was going to buy her a book on communication though. "However, that is where it must remain now. As history." Deeply personal history, but only that nonetheless.

"Gaining weight isn't as easy as it looks—at least for me," she said ignoring his promise and admonition completely.

"I know. That is why I have hired a personal trainer for you."

"Why can't I just use yours?" she demanded. "At least I already know him."

"I thought you would be more comfortable with a woman."

Chloe gave him a knowing look. "You mean *you* would be more comfortable with a female working with me."

"I will not deny it."

"I don't flirt, Ariston."

"This I know."

"So?"

"I am at heart a traditional Greek man." One who had spent enough time talking with his naked ex-wife in his arms.

He pulled her back into his lap, this time draping her legs over his as he insinuated one hand between her thighs. "You are so enticing, *yineka mou.*"

She laughed. "Right. With the dark circles under

my eyes and my underweight body, I hardly look like a woman."

"Never say so. You are the most feminine woman I've ever met. You turn me on." He took her hand and curled it around the hard and leaking proof of his claim.

It felt as if every muscle in his body seized at the touch and he made no effort to stifle his groan of gratification.

"Sometimes I think a stiff breeze could excite you." But her hand squeezed convulsively on his hardness.

"No breezes, only you." And that was more true than he wanted to examine, even within himself. "Regardless, I will not allow your health to suffer carrying my child. On this, I will not be moved."

"You're so darn bossy, you know that, don't you?" Her hand slid up and down his shaft, her eyes going heavy-lidded and a small moan escaping her lips.

He had always reveled in how much she enjoyed touching him.

"I am what I am." He did not consider himself bossy, simply right. "And what I am is a man who needs to be inside you."

She didn't answer, but then he didn't expect her to as he slid his fingers expertly over her clitoris and down until he penetrated her honeyed depths, making her body jolt and her hips cant toward him.

She was wet and hot, so obviously aroused despite her arguments that he had to draw on more self-control than even he thought he had to stop himself taking her that very second. He touched her until her slick dew covered her sex, preparing her completely for his invasion.

When he brought her up to straddle him once again, she tilted her pelvis so her opening pressed against the head of his sex.

"Want you," she moaned as she pressed down to encase him in her drenched heat.

"Yes," he hissed, the barrier of the condom not nearly enough to keep him away from the knife edge of ecstasy.

He slipped his hand between them, pressing gently with his thumb against her clitoris, so every movement of their hips caused her pleasure to spike. She cried out, and begged him not to stop, which he had no intention of doing.

They rocked together, the urgency growing with each deep thrust of his sex inside her welcoming flesh.

"You are mine," he growled, watching her intently.

She looked into his eyes, her own dazed with passion, but no words came out of her mouth.

"Say it," he demanded.

"I'm yours," she gasped out in rapture as she gave the signs that told him she was on the verge of climaxing.

He pressed just a little bit harder with his thumb and shouted his own triumph as she came around him.

Her convulsions sparked his own completion, the only sound coming out of him then a guttural groan as his sex erupted in the condom.

This between them, this at least was right.

Dressed again, Chloe snuggled drowsily in Ariston's arms. "So now I know why you had Angela ride with the security team."

"You have been away from my side for three weeks. We deserved some time alone." Had she not missed him at all?

She'd certainly showed no signs of wanting to get to New York as soon as possible.

"I think we would have survived waiting until tonight to share a bed."

"Perhaps you would have—clearly I was not so content to wait."

"I didn't say I was content." She yawned, cuddling in closer.

He ate it up. He'd always enjoyed his wife's affectionate side...or rather *ex-wife*. Not that she would be that for much longer.

"You have not been sleeping," he censured.

"I've had a lot to do."

"At night?" He did not think so.

"My mind doesn't always shut down when my body wants to."

He did not ask what thoughts had kept her awake. He did not think the answer would make him happy. She'd shown enough reluctance to leave her little coastal town. He'd been forced to come and get her, and therefore had no intention of bringing her worries in this regard to the forefront again.

"Sleep now," he commanded.

She needed it and he needed some space to think.

She nodded, adjusting her position so she was lying across the seat, her head in his lap.

His plan had gone according to his calculations right down the line, until it came to Chloe leaving her home of nearly two years. Then things had gotten more than dicey. She'd thrown a full-fledged spanner in the works.

Three weeks of cajoling his recalcitrant ex-wife into making the move to New York before they were both retirees had convinced Ariston that he needed to change their schedule on certain things.

Mentally going over the list of things they had to do before leaving New York, he brushed his fingers through her hair.

"Mmmm...nice. Don't stop," she slurred as her body relaxed into sleep.

He didn't, finding the action as relaxing as she did.

She was with him now, without arguing.

So, he should be content.

Why wasn't he?

"What do you mean, we're getting married?" Chloe nearly screeched as she waved the contract she'd just finished reading at Ariston.

They were in his office again, his lawyer and the Dioletis attorney in the outer office with Jean. Ariston had insisted Chloe read through the contract in privacy before the lawyers witnessed its signing.

No darn wonder. Far from the contract he'd initially told her she would be signing, this one was a clear prenup, with rather generous financial terms, but an entirely unambiguous clause that gave Ariston majority custody of any future children should Chloe leave him or have an affair.

Presumably any other behavior on her part would not be enough to spur him into filing for divorce. She didn't know what to think.

Ariston, who sat beside her on the sofa they'd made love on her last time in his office, took the papers and set them on the low table in front of them. "I decided there was no reason to hold off on the marriage aspect of our bargain."

"But you said you didn't want to get married again until I had successfully given birth to your child." She wasn't sure she wanted to marry him at all.

"I may not have considered all angles when I made that stipulation."

"You're kidding!"

"I do not joke about matters this serious."

"Right. Contracts are right up there with God in your book."

"My grandfather would not appreciate your blaspheming."

"Takis isn't here."

"No, he is in Greece, eagerly waiting to welcome you back into his family."

Ariston went to brush his hand through her hair and ran into her French twist. His frown looked absolutely thwarted. "I do not like your hair like this."

"I do." Before he could pursue further argument over something so insignificant, she said, "So, this *is* about your grandfather. I knew he wouldn't be happy with the thought that his great-grandchild was to be born out of wedlock."

"I never mentioned that particular aspect of our proposed arrangement to him."

"And you finally realized it would be a bad idea to *ever* do so, didn't you?" she couldn't help taunting.

The man was just too sure he was always right.

"Perhaps."

"There's no perhaps about it."

Ariston was awful at admitting when he was wrong. Probably because the Greek tycoon golden boy so rarely was. There *was* a reason for his arrogance and it wasn't just money and genetics.

"I had many reasons for rethinking my position on the timing for our marriage."

"Did you now?" She wasn't buying it, not for one single solitary minute.

"I did."

"Name them."

"Your health."

"What about my health?" *Sheesh*...he acted as if she was just out of hospital or something.

"It could take months for you to gain back the weight you've lost since the divorce."

"So?"

"So, you will not be getting pregnant until that happens."

"Again, *so?*"

"It occurred to me that putting off the marriage was unnecessary unless I believed you were going to once again cheat me."

"I didn't cheat you—" she began to hotly deny, but he interrupted her.

"So you maintain, but we must agree to disagree on our perception of your actions."

"How magnanimous of you." She wasn't being sarcastic.

For a man of his temperament to agree to disagree was no small concession. The man liked being right almost as much as he liked making money.

"Yes, well…it also occurred to me that you might feel more settled in your return to your normal life with the assurance of a legal bond between us."

"Wasn't the contract going to be the legal bond?" she asked with some confusion, while reeling at the reality he considered their marriage her normal life.

What had the last two years been? Some kind of temporary aberration?

"If there is one thing I have come to understand about you in the past weeks, it is that you and I do not place the same importance on a signed contract."

There was no arguing that point. "So, you've decided we should get married *now?*"

"Yes."

"You didn't think that maybe you should have asked me if that's what I wanted?"

The slight flare in his azure eyes said better than words that clearly he had not. "You had already agreed to the terms."

"Yes, but I didn't expect to become Mrs. Spiridakou in two days' time at the courthouse."

"You never ceased to be Mrs. Spiridakou. You retained my name."

"Yes, but I dropped the *Mrs.* and you know it."

He frowned in acknowledgment of that truth. "Now or later, it should not matter."

"But according to you, it *does* matter to me." He wanted her to feel secure in her life—he'd said so.

It was actually really rather sweet and very thoughtful, further proof that Ariston wasn't exactly like her father used to be. They both might be business sharks, but Ariston had a heart.

Even if he wouldn't admit it. And maybe she wasn't the only one he was thinking needed the bonds of marriage between them.

"Are you refusing to marry me?"

"Are you asking?" she pressed, no longer against the idea, but not ready to give in yet either.

"Are you saying I have to?" His business-shark mask fell away to be replaced by an out-and-out glare.

"Yes."

She didn't care if what they had *was* a business arrangement, they were getting married again. And for her, that was personal. Deeply so.

Giving no clue to what he was about to do, Ariston silently got up from the couch and walked over to his desk. He opened the top drawer and pulled something out before coming back to her.

He stopped at the end of the sofa closest to where she sat. "I am not a romantic man."

"This isn't a matter of romance." For him at least. What her heart got out of it wasn't any of his business, since he'd made it plain that he had no interest in that organ. "It is a matter of respect."

Understanding tinged with relief crossed his masculine features. "In that case…"

He dropped to one knee. Right there, in the middle of his office, on the hand-stitched Turkish carpet.

He lifted the object in his hand toward her and she recognized the jeweler's exclusive and distinctive packaging on what turned out to be a ring box. It wasn't the same jeweler her original engagement and wedding ring had come from. It was the one whose catalog Ariston had found her thumbing through six months after they were married.

She'd told him how much she liked their exclusive line of chocolate diamonds.

He flipped the box open. "Marry me, Chloe."

She reached out to touch the ring. It was a large square-cut chocolate diamond set in yellow gold. Another preference she'd shared with him despite the popularity of platinum amongst their set. On either side of the center stone was a cluster of white diamonds.

"It's beautiful," she whispered in awe.

"Beautiful enough to wear for the rest of your life?" he asked carefully.

That really was the question, wasn't it? Did she want to spend a lifetime with this man? She'd walked away before, believing her love deserved to be returned. She still hoped that one day it would be, but she'd realized something about love in their two years apart.

It wasn't a stingy emotion and it didn't die just because she'd been separated from her beloved.

Ariston had said on her first trip to New York that this was their second chance and she realized she wanted to take it, all the way.

*"Yes."*

He pulled her into a mind-blowing kiss, which was awfully romantic, no matter what he claimed to the contrary.

When they came up for air, she said, "No wonder you didn't take me to that gorgeous apartment you set up for me."

"I thought you would sleep better in our bed. You never seemed to have any trouble before."

They'd spent the night in his Manhattan townhouse, their home while they'd been married. Sleeping in the master bed with him had felt strange, but in retrospect she could see that once his mind had been made up, she'd become his wife again without her even knowing it.

She wasn't about to tell him that it wasn't the comfort or lack thereof of her bed in Oregon that had kept her awake. It didn't matter now. "Having sex had more to do with my long and restful sleep than the comfort of the mattress, Ariston. You tired me out."

He looked quite pleased with that pronouncement.

She ignored his satisfaction and asked. "Are all of my things in the house, then?"

"Your art supplies and personal items, yes. Your furniture is in storage until you decide what you want to do with it."

He really had never intended for her to live in the gorgeous apartment. At least not once his plans for them getting remarried had come into play. She wondered at what point he'd changed his mind on that, and decided to ask.

"After the third phone call in which you put off leaving for New York another day," he replied to her question with more candor than she'd expected.

Maybe more honesty than he'd intended, too, by the look on his handsome face.

He'd been uncertain of her and decided to take measures

not to feel that way again. She'd been right. The wedding wasn't just about making her feel secure—it was about making him feel it, too.

# CHAPTER TEN

CHLOE felt truly lovely for the first time in forever as she stared at her image in the full-length mirror in their bedroom.

She'd donned the champagne cocktail dress Ariston had had altered to fit her perfectly for their courthouse nuptials and brushed her wavy hair until it shone.

The small amount of makeup she'd applied made her green eyes stand out and her bow-shaped lips look kissable.

She was looking forward to Ariston's reaction to that.

Opening the door into the upstairs hall, she heard her husband-to-be's voice mixed with tones she recognized but would never have expected to hear in this venue. Not ever.

Takis Spiridakou had flown over from Greece to see them wed. She knew it.

Flying down the stairs, she yelled his name. "Takis!"

He spun to face her and put his arms out. "Pappous, child. How many times must I tell you? I am your *pappous.*"

She threw herself against him, though still mindful of what she knew about his health.

He hugged her tightly and she hugged him back, moisture gathering in her eyes. "It is so good to see you. Ariston didn't tell me you were coming."

"It was my surprise to both of you." Takis kissed both

her cheeks in greeting before grinning at her, his face lined but still handsome like his grandson. "I am determined to witness this civil ceremony. I did not the last time and look what happened."

Chloe choked on her laughter, but she didn't tell him his being at the other wedding wouldn't have mattered. Takis would not only be offended, but he absolutely wouldn't believe her.

Ariston had come by his arrogance honestly.

The doorbell rang before any more could be said. Seconds later, the sounds of Rhea's, Samuel's and Chloe's father's voices could be heard.

"Takis! I did not know you would be here," Eber Dioletis said with an expansive smile.

The elder Spiridakou did not return it. "You think I am a deaf fool living my life in our home country, Eber? Heh?"

"I don't know what you mean," Chloe's father replied cautiously, looking much older than when she'd last seen him.

"You don't, heh? So, it was some other blind fool who tried to marry my grandson's wife off to another man?"

"Now, Takis—" Eber started.

But Takis was having none of it. He pointed a slightly trembling finger at the other retired businessman. "You listen to me, that girl is my family. You try to undermine that again, it will be more than a few contracts you lose."

Takis might suffer a fine tremor in his limbs, but he wasn't the least bit stooped with age and made a hugely imposing figure.

Everyone wore identical expressions of amazement at the threat and all that his words implied. Everyone but Chloe.

She wasn't surprised at all. Underneath the warmth of family love that Takis Spiridakou wore with such ease was a man who could both run Spiridakou & Sons Enterprises *and* teach Ariston to be the business shark that he was.

Her beloved old man had a titanium spine and her father would do well to remember it.

Warmth spread through Chloe at the realization that she'd never been as alone as she'd felt. She turned to meet her father's still gaping countenance.

From her position of security with both these amazing Spiridakou men at her back, she extended her hand in welcome. "Father."

"Ariston thought you would want me here," he said almost diffidently, grasping her hand and holding on rather than shaking it.

"He was right." She smiled up at her soon-to-be-again husband while extricating her hand from her father's hold. "Thank you."

"When you told me of the healing nature of your last phone call, I thought you would want a chance to see him in person."

"You were right."

Ariston preened under the pronouncement and she found herself smiling even as her father hugged her and whispered the second "I'm sorry" of his life toward her along with an emotional declaration of fatherly love.

Perhaps even old business sharks really could change.

She hugged him back and told him she loved him too, but then grinned. "That doesn't make me any less happy to hear Pappous made sure the company paid for you thinking I was just one of its assets, though."

Her father gasped, but Rhea just laughed. "You all forget that while Chloe's a lot more like Mom than I am, she still carries our dad's genetics."

At that, her father looked proud if still a little shocked. Ariston didn't look surprised though and Chloe hadn't expected him to. He'd already commented on the fact that she had a ruthless streak even she hadn't been aware of.

He said now, "It is something I have come to appreciate as true."

"Oh, really?" she asked.

"Yes. You knew what you wanted and you went after it."

She wasn't sure how he came by that conclusion, unless he was talking about how determined she'd been to save Rhea's marriage. She didn't deny it though, because she, at least, knew it was true.

"That sounds more like you than my father," she teased.

"He and I are not so unalike."

Chloe had to look away at that reminder. She believed that their differences were enough that she wasn't setting herself up for a lifetime of hurts like her mother had endured. If she was wrong, neither of them were going to come out unscathed.

The prenup had pretty much guaranteed that for Ariston.

"Enough talk. Let us have a glass of ouzo to celebrate this day and then get this wedding on the road." Takis brandished a bottle he'd no doubt brought all the way from the home country.

Like the first time five years ago for their courthouse wedding, the court came to them.

The same Supreme Court judge, who was an old friend of her father's, arrived to preside over the civil ceremony. Minutes later, the two lawyers who had witnessed the signing of the prenuptial agreement joined them.

As Chloe looked around the room, she realized the players were all the same as five years ago.

Takis was the only person who had not been in this very room before to witness an identical ceremony.

It was all the same. Soft strains of classical music played in the background, just like before. Another buffet luncheon was laid out on the sideboard of the dining room for after the ceremony. Not so much as a lamp had changed in the decor of this room either.

As her sense of déjà vu grew, the hope and security that had buoyed Chloe up bled from her in a steady, inexorable stream. Why did she think this was going to work any better than it had the first time around?

Because she was more aware? Less naively hopeful that Ariston would fall in love with her?

Her gaze slid to Takis Spiridakou. The reason for this event. Had he not stubbornly refused to acknowledge the divorce between her and Ariston, her ex-husband would have gone looking elsewhere for a mother to his children.

Chloe was honest enough with herself to admit that reading in the society pages about Ariston marrying another woman and giving her children would have killed her. It was time for a little more honesty as well.

She wasn't marrying him for Rhea's sake or that of the employees at Dioletis Industries.

No, agreeing to this marriage was all down to her.

And ultimately, no matter what came of it, she'd agreed for one reason and one reason only—her abiding love for the Greek billionaire.

In that moment, Chloe realized one player in this drama was very much changed.

Her.

She knew what she was agreeing to. Period. And this time around she wasn't doing it for her family, nor even for her own naive belief that somehow, some way her billionaire husband was going to fall in love with her.

She was doing it because *she* loved *him* and even if he wanted to believe otherwise, Ariston had a heart and if anyone was getting a crack at it, that person was going to be her.

She might not get everything she wanted from this marriage, but she would get more than a lifetime of loneliness in love with a man forever lost to her. Another woman might see that as a deal breaker, but then what another woman might do wasn't important to Chloe.

She knew what she was willing to do to pursue her own happiness and she wasn't a coward to shy away from the risks involved. That was something her mother had taught her.

Her parents hadn't had an ideal marriage, but her mom had never expressed a desire to be anywhere than where she was. Chloe hadn't understood that. She'd thought her father should have been a better husband, and even he acknowledged that now, but ultimately her mother had been strong enough to go after what she wanted.

Ariston was right about one thing—Chloe was, too.

Today might not be the joyous occasion of two people deeply in love pledging their lives together, but it wasn't a funeral either.

It was a chance at the future—a chance Ariston had invited her to take and one she knew was necessary.

Necessary for Ariston to please the one person on this earth he held any true love for. For Takis to find contentment in his waning years, knowing his family would go into the next generation. A requirement for the survival of Dioletis Industries. Necessary for the renewal of her sister's love-based marriage.

But definitely, and most important to her decision to go through with it, this marriage was necessary for Chloe's best hope at a future.

Her mother had once told her that just as only some were born to greatness, not all were meant to have common domestic bliss. She'd been talking about her own marriage, Chloe had realized as she'd gotten older.

Her mother had accepted that she would never have a husband who put her first, but she had not railed against her fate. She'd accepted it with a grace Chloe was determined to emulate. Because she finally realized that in her own way, her mother had also been quite happy.

Yes, marriage to a man like Eber couldn't have been easy, but Chloe now knew that her mother had been a strong woman. And if that marriage wasn't what she wanted, she would have walked away from it.

"Chloe." A hand landed on her shoulder, her sister's concerned gaze fixed on Chloe. "Are you all right? Ariston's been trying to get your attention."

She looked past Rhea to Ariston. "I'm sorry, did you say something? I was thinking."

"His Honor is ready to begin," Ariston said, his tone questioning, his expression almost grim.

Chloe ignored both and nodded her understanding.

The judge indicated where they should stand and Chloe went to take her place beside Ariston. With hands like ice, Chloe spoke her vows with conviction if not a surplus of emotion.

Ariston wasn't interested in her love, and right now she wasn't offering it to him on a plate either.

As Ariston had said, this was no great romantic moment. But it was a necessary moment.

Her beautiful Chanel dress was a prop, not a tender gift from an eager groom. Still, it would look good in the photos that would no doubt be released later to specific newspapers and glossy magazines.

She'd learned the smile she would wear in them, for the world to see, in her early childhood when her father had paraded his family for the sake of his public image and that of his business.

She chatted adroitly with their guests over lunch and

managed in every way not to let herself down over the next hours.

Later, when everyone but Takis had left, Chloe allowed herself a modicum of relaxing in her guard.

The old man looked over-the-top pleased with the outcome of the day.

Ariston had disappeared into his office to make some calls, once again wearing his enigmatic tycoon mask. Not that Chloe had expected anything different. Today was about a business deal for him.

She turned to the old man. "It looks like it's just you and me. Would you like to play a game of checkers?"

She'd found a fellow lover of the simple game soon after meeting Takis five years ago. They had whiled away many an hour in his home in Greece similarly occupied.

"Now, that is a pleasure I have not had in two years."

"Only maybe I should change out of my wedding finery," she said with an ironic twist of her lips.

"Nonsense. What man could resist playing checkers with a woman dressed to the nines, heh?"

She laughed softly, but took her place at the small square game table in the corner of the living room.

"Does my grandson play with you?"

"He used to, before."

"Then he will again. That is a good thing, child."

She nodded with a slight smile, unsure how much it could really signify.

She and the old man had both played their opening gambits when Takis spoke again. "My Helene, God rest her soul, she and I married at the behest of our parents. Did you know?"

"No." But that explained his insistence on seeing the most positive side of her marriage to Ariston.

On his pressuring Ariston into an arranged marriage

to begin with. By all accounts, Takis and Helene had been very happy together.

"We had forty good years together before the cancer took her." His face suffused with melancholy for a brief moment as he paused with his hand over the checkerboard. "She was the light in my life for all that time."

Chloe smiled, having no difficulty believing his claim.

Takis made his move and then looked up, his gaze very serious. "Words of love were never spoken between us."

"But you were so happy."

"We were."

"You must have loved her." Chloe frowned, unable to imagine a man not loving the woman he considered the light of his life.

*"Ne."* Yes. He'd agreed.

"But you never told her." Why wouldn't he?

"I did not need to. She knew she was my wife, that our marriage vows were sacred to me."

"You don't think she minded, that you never said the words?"

"She never said them either, child."

"But…"

"My son, Balios, now…he has imagined himself in love many times and married almost all of them. Though he has only managed to give me one grandchild." Takis shook his head at his son's failings.

Chloe's mouth twisted with distaste she found difficult to suppress whenever she thought of the selfish man that was Ariston's father. "I don't think what Balios calls love is what most of us would associate with that emotion."

"Perhaps. What I am sure of, child, is that mutual benefit and compatible backgrounds can be the best basis for marriage." Because he'd experienced it, he believed it.

"Not everyone is as lucky as you and Helene."

"You and my grandson will be, now that this nonsense of a divorce is behind you."

"If he'd loved me, I wouldn't have left him," she admitted. "And he certainly wouldn't have divorced me."

Or had the papers drawn up for her father to discover.

"You think so? His father has divorced every one of the wives he *loved*."

It was a valid point.

"You're sure our marriage will make it this time?"

"Yes."

"Why so certain?" she asked jokingly, expecting another rendition of the I-was-here-to-witness-the-ceremony theme.

"My grandson has grown up."

"He was hardly a child before." At thirty, he'd already been working for Spiridakou & Sons Enterprises for most of his life, having started running errands within the company for his grandfather at the age of twelve. Ariston had been in charge of operations for seven years by the time he divorced her. "I don't see how two years could have made that much difference."

"Didn't it with you?" Takis asked as he kinged one of his pieces.

"Yes," she had to admit. She'd only today realized how much. She jumped two of his pieces with relish.

"Two years ago you got on a plane and flew out of my grandson's life without a word. You won't do that again."

"No. I won't."

"See? You've grown up."

"You're a very stubborn man, Takis Spiridakou." And he liked to be right.

Just like his grandson.

"This is not news to me, child. A man never built a

life worth having by giving in on everything that mattered to him."

"I suppose you think that goes for women as well."

"Why wouldn't I?"

"I'm not sure what Ariston would do if I turned out to be as stubborn as his beloved *pappous*," she said with the first real smile in hours.

"I am terrified to contemplate it, though after the past weeks, I had begun to suspect such already." Ariston came to stand beside Chloe's chair and laid his hand on her nape, under the fall of her hair.

That simple touch felt so right.

She looked up at Ariston, trying to read the odd expression on his chiseled features. "I didn't hear you come in."

"You and Pappous were in deep conversation, not to mention playing your favorite game."

"It's a child's game, I know," she admitted.

Takis glared at her, his expression affronted. "I will have you know it is the game of ancient kings."

"It's sold in the children's toy department, not the section reserved for royalty," she countered, relishing the old argument.

Takis opened his mouth to retort, but Ariston put up his hand. "Truce, you two. You'll have far more enjoyment playing the game than arguing about it."

"Are you sure about that?" she asked. "Your grandfather loves to argue."

"This is true."

That earned them both a censorious frown from the old man. "It is a good thing for both of you that I hold you so dear."

"Are you saying you love me, Pappous?" she had the temerity to ask with humor.

He went very serious to answer. "The words do not need to be spoken to be felt."

He believed that with every fiber of his being, she could tell, but she wasn't as tranquil on the subject. She didn't know if she ever would be.

"I have a little surprise for you two," Takis announced.

"Your arrival this morning was not surprise enough?" Ariston asked with a warm smile for the old man.

"It is because of my arrival that I have arranged this." Takis produced a hotel key card and brandished it with the air of a man conjuring the golden rings that had disappeared from the stage.

"You will not stay in a hotel. You will stay here, with family," Ariston proclaimed, no give in his tone or his stance.

"But naturally. The hotel room is for you and your lovely wife. Newlyweds should not spend their first night of marriage under the same roof as their grandfather."

"I thought you did not recognize our divorce," Chloe teased, strangely disconcerted about using that key card. "We can hardly be newlyweds, then."

It added a romantic tone to the day that she'd been trying very hard to acknowledge as unnecessary under the circumstances.

"*Ohi,* no more do I, but I am not so set in my ways, I do not recognize a recommitment when I witness one."

Chloe almost laughed at the old man's absolute intransigence on the subject.

Ariston showed no hesitancy however as he accepted the gift with a bussing on both his grandfather's cheeks and warm thanks. "Where are we going, then?"

"Only the best hotel in the city. I would accept nothing less for my grandson and his bride," Takis promised.

# CHAPTER ELEVEN

CHLOE discovered how very right Takis was as they were shown into one of the hotel's premier suites.

Not only was it richly appointed and impeccably decorated, but it was bigger than her apartment back in Oregon. The dining table had seating for six and the living area could have hosted a small party easily.

She let out a low whistle of appreciation. "Your grandfather certainly knows how to live in luxury, doesn't he?"

"He worked hard to be where he is and his father before him. Should he book us into a motel?"

"I'm surprised you even know that there are motels in the city." She wouldn't have five years ago, when they'd first met and she'd known nothing of life beyond the pampered if lonely existence of her childhood.

"When I researched the hospitality industry before venturing into it, I made sure I looked at every type of accommodation available to suit every strata of society."

"You've diversified into the hospitality industry?"

"I'd begun the move soon after our marriage. SSE now owns and operates a line of exclusive cruise ships."

"You never told me about it." Not that he'd made it a habit to discuss business with her, but he'd been far more free with information about SSE than her father had ever been about Dioletis Industries at home.

"I meant to name the ships after our children."

"But we didn't have any."

"No." He shrugged, the casual movement belying the regret in his eyes. "It was a grandiose idea considering the fact we had not even conceived a child yet when I commissioned the first two ships for building."

"How many are in your fleet now?" she asked, unable to help the awe she felt at such a huge venture.

Cruise ships were like small cities. Building one would be a big enough endeavor—to have started his fleet with two had shown how committed he'd been to the enterprise.

"Ten. We have three different routes in the Mediterranean, all of which sail out of or land in Piraeus."

"I'm not surprised. Greece is home, no matter what your passport says."

He shook his head. "It was a solid business move."

"Oh, yes?" she asked in a teasing tone, not really believing it.

"Very much so. Did you know that Greece took in more tourist dollars than any country in the EU last year?"

"No." And she wouldn't have expected it either.

"Where there is a will and a modicum of intelligence, there is always a way to make money."

"Don't tell my father that."

"He knows my feelings on the subject. I told him investing in bonds and banks was foolish five years ago, but he did not listen to me."

"So, what did you name the ships?" she asked, not really wanting to discuss her father's business failings.

"They are named for the Greek gods of mythology."

She smirked. "Not exactly original."

"No, but popular with the guests."

"Where do the rest of your fleet sail?"

"Two out of Amsterdam, one to Alaska, one to Hawaii,

two in the Caribbean and one to Mexico out of L.A. We hope to commission three more ships next year."

"What does your grandfather think of them?"

"He says they aren't as pretty as our cargo ships, but they'll do."

She laughed, the sound so genuine, it startled her. "That sounds like him."

This was what she and Ariston were like together. It wouldn't be easy to remember that their compatibility didn't mean they were destined to fall in love.

But they *were* good together and it didn't hurt to remember that, too.

When he reached for her, she went to him without hesitation though. This was what they were good at. She and Ariston undressed each other, touching in ways they'd learned in the three years of marriage and the few times they'd been together intimately since then.

She led him toward the bed, her hand wrapped boldly around his erection.

"You are a temptress," he offered gutturally as he pulled her back onto the soft mattress with him.

"Do I tempt you?" she asked as she stroked him up and down, her rhythm stuttering as his fingers found intimate places.

"*Ne.* More than any other woman ever has," he ground out.

Then he burst into movement, rolling them over, so she was under him.

"We are even."

He kissed her passionately and then moved down her body to torment each erogenous spot with his mouth, using lips, tongue and teeth to devastating effect.

She was getting lost in the pleasure but that wasn't what she wanted right now. She needed to prove to him that in this they truly were equal, even if their emotions never would be.

She pushed at his chest. "Let me."

"Let you what, *yineka mou?*"

"I want to touch and taste. It's my turn."

"But I am enjoying myself."

"So, enjoy being tasted."

Finally what she was offering must have clicked, because he rolled off her and offered himself with an alacrity she wasn't sure she would have been capable of.

"I am at your disposal." The remark would have been flip but for the husky quality to his voice.

"Thank you."

"I am certain, sweet one, that it is I who will soon be thanking you. Profusely."

She smiled and loved that he could still do that—make sex fun. Even after everything that had gone on between them.

She knelt between his thighs, rubbing against her own aching nipples, trying to soothe the need for his touch.

His nostrils flared and his eyelids dropped to half-mast. "You are so damn sexy."

"Glad you think so." She caressed his inner thighs with both hands, gently guiding his legs a little farther apart.

He bit off a sound of pleasure at that simple touch and satisfaction coursed through her. In this, he was hers.

She gently cupped his heavy scrotum sac with one hand, carefully rolling the balls as his shaft grew harder, pointing toward his stomach, viscous fluid beading at the tip.

"Is this still one of your favorite spots to be touched?" she wondered aloud as she slid her other fingers behind to caress his perineum.

The way his body jolted at the first light caress to the soft skin between the base of his balls and his backside said he did. She pressed in a little, looking for a bigger reaction and got it when he groaned long and low. "That feels so good."

"I can tell."

He smiled at her, pleasure warming the azure of his eyes.

"I know what will feel even better," he hinted.

"So do I." And with that, she dropped forward and placed an openmouthed kiss on the underside of his sex, just under the head.

It was the most sensitive spot on his penis and he used to go nuts when she would drag her teeth along it so lightly the touch was barely there.

"Please." His husky tone went straight to her core.

She took the mushroom-shaped head into her mouth, hit with the familiarity of his taste in a visceral way she had not expected. Memories and feelings rushed through her, taking away her sense of time and the present. She enjoyed him in a way she had not done since seeing him again three weeks ago.

On purpose. She knew what doing this for him did to her. It was one of the few times he truly allowed himself to become vulnerable, that he let her direct the pleasure between them.

The way his hips moved, the sounds he made…it all melded together in her mind and her heart. She reveled in it, knowing he could not see the emotion pouring through her as she took him to the brink.

He tried to push her head away. "Stop. I can't hold back," he gasped out.

She wanted to ignore him, but he wouldn't kiss her after if he came in her mouth. And she wanted the drugging kisses only he could give her.

She pulled back, crawling up his body. "I know you

can hold it back until I come. After all, you are Ariston Spiridakou."

"That may be, but still I am only a man." His cerulean gaze was dark with need.

"Never say so," she teased as her body taunted him with barely there entry.

"The condom," he bit out.

She would have argued, but right then, a small barrier between them would be welcome. Keeping the deepest of her emotions locked down and holding back words of love was taking all the strength she could manage.

She concentrated on the task fully as she rolled the condom down his engorged flesh. He moaned and a small smile of satisfaction flirted at the corners of her mouth.

"I see that smile," he said in an accusing tone.

She looked up, careful to keep her emotions from her eyes. "I like making you react."

"I had noticed." His expression was filled with feral intensity that she used to mistake for the beginnings of love.

She would not make that mistake this time around.

She crawled back up his body, seating him inside her in one downward thrust.

She cried out at the intensity of pleasure. So full and connected. She let her eyelids fall shut lest she reveal how profound this moment was to her.

The first time they'd made love—at least love for her—as a married couple in two years. It was beyond intense; it was earth-shattering.

He grabbed her hips, stopping her from moving. "Are you all right?"

She nodded, her throat too tight to speak right then.

"Open your eyes," he commanded.

That she could not do. She shook her head.

"Yes, *yineka mou,* give me the pleasure of seeing your pleasure in that beautiful emerald-green."

"Feels too good," she managed.

"Let me see."

She just shook her head and started moving. His body went rigid under her and he moaned. "Stop."

"No." She made no attempt to establish a smooth rhythm, just moved up and down, feeding the bliss between them with ever-spiraling strength.

He thrust upward, his hold on her hips fighting her for control. She adjusted and moaned as ecstasy drew closer with each movement of their bodies.

He used his hold on her hips and the upward cant of his own hips to make sure his pelvis put pressure against her swollen clitoris each time their bodies came fully together. She cried out as her climax built to unbearable heights. She was right on the edge and she could not go over.

"Open your eyes," he demanded again.

This time she could do nothing but obey and at the look of atavistic lust in his eyes, felt herself soaring over the precipice. Her body convulsed as a sensual moan exploded out of her.

He gave one last, powerful thrust upward and then shouted as his body went rigid and his own climax took him, their gazes never breaking contact.

But when she felt words of love bubbling forth, she let herself fall forward, severing the tie between their souls before it revealed too much.

Ariston held his wife close to his body and listened to the soft sounds of her breathing.

The consummation of their marriage had been amazing, as had the very sexy bath that followed. She'd fallen asleep almost as soon as they'd climbed back into a freshly made bed.

He'd called housekeeping before following her into the luxurious bathroom complete with a whirlpool tub. His lovely wife had shown her appreciation for his thoughtfulness with a very thorough kiss before tucking herself into his body and going boneless in rest.

He had not been so lucky. Sleep eluded him as memories of their lovemaking taunted him.

She'd been holding something back, a part of her he could not touch, no matter how intense the pleasure.

It brought back memories of the final months of their marriage and he realized one of the reasons he'd been so sure she wanted out was this distance she'd kept between them.

Distance that had not been there in the beginning.

He understood it even less now than he had before. Why keep part of herself back from him when he wanted it all? When at one point, she'd willingly given him everything? Though he did not believe in love, he did believe she'd thought herself in love with him in the beginning.

Something had changed though. He just did not know what.

He would have considered that it might have been another man, but she showed not even the slightest signs in that direction.

Chloe might have cheated their contract, but she was not an adulterer. Of that he was absolutely certain.

He was not the sort of man to compromise and had realized early in his marriage that he was far more possessive than he'd ever suspected. His need to be with her and know she preferred his company over any other had bothered him, made him feel weak.

Chloe didn't flirt with other men though. She didn't

ask to spend weeks on shopping excursions in Europe as many wives in their set did, but she held something indefinable back.

And it raised that sense of possession, disturbing his equilibrium.

Until he knew why she felt that need...strike that, *knowing why was not good enough.* Until she gave him everything, held nothing back and did not seek to create distance between them, he would not be content.

She had developed more interests outside their time together in the last year of their marriage. She'd been less available to him and he had discovered he did not like that at all either.

Again, her desire to spend more time away from him had made it all the easier to believe Chloe didn't want to be married to him in the first place, and had plotted to keep the relationship short-lived when he discovered the birth control.

His grandfather had told him to learn to live with it when Ariston had complained how much time Chloe's outside interests seem to take from her. Pappous had said that she deserved to have her own life.

Ariston was busy enough with his work—she needed her own pursuits so she would not resent the time he spent with Spiridakou & Sons Enterprises.

Remembering that conversation, Ariston had taken steps to give Chloe what she needed, but now he wondered if he'd made a mistake buying her a New York art gallery. Would she use it as an excuse to spend more time away from him, maintaining the distance he hated and she seemed to want?

At least for the next ten days, he had no such worries. He'd arranged for them to sail on one of his cruise ships, a ten-day excursion in the Mediterranean.

Chloe had expressed interest in exploring the other, less populated islands of Greece, when they were married before. He knew she would enjoy this cruise.

He would just have to worry about whether to fess up to buying the gallery when they returned to New York—once they'd returned from their second honeymoon. Not that she would not learn the truth eventually.

The gallery was already in her name.

Until then, he would do his best to break down the wall she seemed intent on erecting between them.

# CHAPTER TWELVE

CHLOE stood on the balcony of Ariston's personal suite on his ship, the *Colossus*.

How appropriate that they were docking in Rhodes tomorrow.

She'd been shocked when he'd informed her that he'd arranged for them to take a cruise to celebrate their remarriage. They would fly to Piraeus and sail from that port. For a guy who insisted this was purely a business arrangement and better for being so, the man had a hugely romantic streak.

He'd said no romance, but two dozen peach roses, her favorite, filled their suite with delectable fragrance and a bottle of celebratory champagne—her favorite vintage—had greeted them on arrival.

He was pulling out all the stops, but she didn't know why. What more did he hope to gain?

He already had her agreement to give him the children Takis was so keen on spoiling. It was Ariston who insisted they use condoms until she'd gained a minimum of ten pounds.

Maybe that was what this cruise was about? The way they were fed, she was going to gain at least five pounds in the next ten days.

And she wasn't doing it with the healthiest alternatives either. Ariston had left both their personal trainers behind.

He never traveled without his, but when she'd asked him about it, he'd said it was their honeymoon. As if that was an answer.

When their marriage was about anything but romance.

The skirt of her green dress fluttered around her legs from the wind coming off the Mediterranean. She'd loved the dress when they'd seen it in the boutique, but didn't think she'd wear it as often in the longer length.

So, Ariston had had it altered to mid-calf and she loved the way it made her feel. Both his attention and the gorgeous cut of the dress that disguised her deficiencies and played up her figure's positives.

She had to work doubly hard to maintain her perspective when it felt like Ariston was doing everything in his power to undermine her careful intentions.

"What has you thinking so seriously?" he asked as warm, muscular arms came around her.

"Nothing, really. Just watching the ocean."

"Yes?"

"I'm really enjoying this cruise, Ariston. Thank you for taking the time to make it happen."

"You are welcome. It does not bother you that I spend a couple of hours each morning keeping track of my business?"

Truthfully? She relished it. She needed a break from him to shore up her defenses every day. They were close enough to crumbling as it was.

"No, of course not. SSE will not run itself."

"No." There was a quality to his voice she did not understand.

"How is the takeover of Dioletis Industries coming?"

"I prefer *merger.* And it is going according to plan. Your sister seems quite pleased."

"She has no reason not to be."

He turned Chloe in his arms so their eyes met. "And you? Do you have any reasons to be less than pleased?"

"No."

"You are certain." His gaze was far too penetrating for comfort.

She looked away. "Yes, of course."

"That is the classic indication one is telling a lie."

Her gaze flew back to his. "What?"

"To look away before or during speech."

"Well, I'm not lying." Just uncomfortable discussing how very happy with her circumstances she was.

She shouldn't *be* this happy, but there was no denying that she was.

"So, you would not undo our marriage if you could?"

"What?" Had he lost his mind? "No!"

"You were coerced."

"That didn't seem to matter to you when you were doing it." And now was a very odd time for him to be having second thoughts on his tactics.

"I have come to appreciate that it would be more pleasant for both of us if you were as content to be married to me as I am to be married to you."

Content? What a weak word, though something loosened in her chest at his claim to it.

"I'm more than content," she said with more honesty than maybe he deserved. "I'm *happy.*"

"Yes?"

"Yes," she said firmly.

"You are not a clingy woman."

Where was this coming from? "No."

"You are more than happy to spend time away from me, even on our honeymoon?"

Oh, for heaven's sake. Was this about his ego? "You are spending no more than a couple of hours on your computer, maybe another on the phone. Considering the work hours you normally keep, I've felt very privileged you give so little time to SSE each day. It would be really churlish of me to complain about it."

"Oh. I see. That is good. I am glad you are not feeling neglected."

She moved closer, until their bodies touched. "I wouldn't say no if you wanted to show how very much you aren't neglecting me again."

"In this, we are very compatible, are we not?" he asked with the air of a man trying to work something out in his head.

"Unbelievably so, really, when you consider how we came to be together."

Instead of kissing her like she hoped and pretty much expected, he stepped back. "It bothers you that our marriage is the result of a business arrangement."

"We already had this discussion."

"And I explained to you that it is a better basis for marriage than so-called *love*."

"In your opinion."

"But not yours."

She saw the trap almost too late. If she said no, he'd wonder why she'd been willing to marry him despite her beliefs. It was only one step farther for him to realize she was in love with him, always had been, and always would be.

"I agreed to this marriage and I don't regret it."

"That is not an answer."

"It certainly is, even if it's not the one you wanted.

Even you, Ariston Spiridakou, cannot always get what
you want."

His gorgeous blue eyes narrowed. "Do not be too certain of that, *yineka mou.* I am very good at getting what
I desire."

A shiver of apprehension ran down her spine, but he
gave her no chance to regroup, sweeping her into the mind-
numbing kiss she'd expected moments ago.

They walked into Rhodes from the cruise ship docks just
like everyone else.

Chloe was amazed by the sight of the city before they
even got beyond the ancient outer wall. "This is incredible. The wall goes all around the city?" she asked Ariston.

"The old town, yes. You will enjoy the marketplace,
especially the artist in you."

"I'm not much of an artist."

"You have talent."

"Some," she agreed. Not enough to dedicate her life to
it, but enough to enjoy losing herself in painting.

"More than a little, but certainly enough of an artist's
soul, regardless, to appreciate the rich texture of this port."

"You've been here before?"

"I've been to all the ports my ships dock. Though I'd
been here years ago, with Pappous as a child on holiday."

"From your tone you have fond memories."

"All my good childhood memories are from times spent
with my grandfather."

"He is a wonderful man."

"Yes."

Ariston was right about the market. It was so busy, so
many shops with a plethora of color and imagery. The
juxtaposition of a modern eatery only a few feet from a

centuries-old fountain still cascading water kept her snapping photo after photo.

She caught sight of a painting in one of the shop windows. It was of the view from the Rhodes harbor and done by an artist who clearly loved his subject matter.

When Ariston noticed her admiring it, he wanted to go inside to purchase it. She nodded at him, waving him away as she crouched to get a shot of a small child playing in the water of the fountain.

When she stood up, one of the security team stood at a discreet distance, but Ariston had gone. The sun was already high in the sky and Chloe felt the wave of heat press down on her. They'd been shopping since early morning.

She approached the outdoor café, thinking a cold drink sounded good right about then. Two men were in charge of luring patrons and seating them.

One of them approached her, a glimmer of devilment in his dark gaze that she couldn't help but appreciate. "You would like to take a seat out of the sun, miss?"

"Yes."

"A table," he said with a wave of his hand to his helper. "For one?"

She shook her head. "Two, please."

She knew from experience, the security team would refuse to sit down themselves. The area was too crowded and they would feel hampered by the confines of space.

"Ah, so you do not travel alone? I thought we could find a nice Rhodesian husband for you." That glimmer of devilment had developed into a full-grown teasing grin.

She laughed, knowing it was part of the charm and maybe even shtick of the place.

"That will not be necessary," came in clipped Greek.

She turned to share her smile with Ariston only to find him glaring at the hapless café host.

The man stepped back a respectful distance. "Of course not, sir. Your table is just this way."

"You are thirsty?" Ariston asked rather than reply, or move toward the table.

"I am." She took his arm and tugged. "And you can either have a refreshment with me or stand glowering in the square. I know which I'd prefer."

"Since you are pulling me along like a cart, I will assume it is my company."

"Yes, though right this second, I'm not sure why."

"He offered to get you a husband." Irritation more than laced his voice—it drowned it.

"It was a joke, Ariston. The rock you put on my finger is big enough for even the visually challenged to spot."

"I thought you liked your ring."

"Oh, for goodness'…I *love* my ring. Now, will you please sit down and order us both some fresh lemonade?"

For once, her oh-so-powerful husband did exactly as he was told. The host himself brought their drinks with a wink for her and a respectful salute to Ariston.

She managed to stifle her giggle, but her smile wasn't going anywhere.

Ariston finally matched it. "You are enjoying yourself."

"More than I can possibly say."

"I am very glad."

"You are a wonderfully attentive husband, Ariston. Thank you."

"It comes with the job description, I think."

"But you do it better than most I've seen." And always had, love or no love.

He preened under the compliment, but kept any arrogant remarks to himself. Full points for the billionaire tycoon on that one.

* * *

Santorini was every bit as magical in its pristine blue and white beauty as she'd expected it to be.

The steep ride up the cliff in the cable car made her nervous, but even Ariston couldn't cajole her into riding a smelly donkey up the switchbacked trail to the same destination.

They ate dinner at a small restaurant overlooking the harbor, the view of the cruise ships spectacular. "*Colossus* is truly that, isn't it?"

Ariston nodded with proud satisfaction. "My fleet of ships are some of the largest sailing the cruise routes."

"Well, if the *Colossus* is anything to go by, they're incredibly luxurious, as well."

"It is my intention that each guest to sail on the Spiridakou fleet feel pampered and outside of their normal life."

"I certainly do."

He grinned. "If I can effect that for a billionaire's wife, then I consider my goal accomplished."

She didn't mention that she'd been living like a small-town business owner the past two years. The truth was, even Ariston's lifestyle had no chance of spoiling her like the staff on the cruise ship had.

"Tomorrow, we go to Crete?"

"Yes. We will go on a tour of the island just like the other tourists," he said with some satisfaction.

She smiled wryly. "Other tourists don't travel with a security detail."

He shrugged.

And really, what could be said? Ariston had lived his whole life with bodyguards watching his every movement, and they were only more necessary now that he'd taken the company so much farther than his grandfather.

\* \* \*

Walking the streets of Kusadasi, Turkey, their final day in port, Chloe had all but given up on trying to keep her emotional distance from Ariston.

She'd managed to hold back words of love, but that was about it.

Treating her with all the consideration and even open affection of any new husband for his bride, Ariston made it too hard for her to maintain her defenses.

While touring the ruins of ancient Ephesus that morning, they'd been asked by several people if they were newlyweds. Because they behaved like it, not like two people who had agreed with cold calculation to a business deal.

He'd taken pains to read up on the ruins and acted as her personal tour guide through the ancient city. She'd been more than charmed; she'd been bowled over by his consideration and forethought.

This man didn't have time for stuff like that, yet he'd made it…for her. What did it all mean?

She'd been determined not to speculate on that particular question this time around, but like with most everything else in regard to her husband, Chloe's intentions had gone flying out the window.

Each day of their *honeymoon,* she fell more deeply under the spell that was Ariston and couldn't even make herself worry about how deeply in love she was with her husband.

"Would you like to buy a rug for the foyer in the townhouse?" Ariston asked, interrupting her thoughts.

He'd stopped in front of one of the shops that sold the hand-stitched carpets the Turkish people were so well known for. She knew exactly which patterned rug in the window had caught her husband's eyes. It was a traditional pattern with dark burgundy the dominant color, and she was almost positive that it was the silk weave, rather than polished cotton.

She learned she was right a few minutes later when they'd been seated and offered the traditional apple tea.

Their salesman, nephew to the man who owned the shop, asked politely after their family and welfare before asking if there was a particular carpet that had caught their eye.

When Ariston told him which he'd like to see, the salesman's eyes lit up. "Ah, a very fine choice. The weave is very tight—the silk will last three hundred years or more."

He waved at a younger man he introduced as his younger cousin. "Show these fine people our beautiful carpets, Achim."

Soon carpets were twirling and landing at their feet on the floor, each angle showing a different intensity to the pattern's colors. Because a Turkish rug merchant never showed just one carpet—he provided comparisons and options in abundance. She'd learned that on their first trip to Turkey.

Just as enthralled by the display as she'd been the first time she'd seen such a thing on their original honeymoon, Chloe sipped delicately at her hot beverage and soaked in the experience.

When one very similar to the carpet in the window, but in a larger size, landed on the pile in front of them, she knew they'd found the one for their home.

Ariston appeared to agree, asking to see that particular carpet up close. Then the haggling began and at the end of it, Chloe was doing all she could not to smack both her husband and the salesman upside the head.

As they left the shop, she demanded, "Was that really necessary? You two spent more than half the time arguing over a difference of a few dollars. You could have paid full price and not even noticed the blip in your checkbook."

"I do not keep a checkbook. Everything is electronic or cash nowadays, *yineka mou.*"

"That's not the point and you know it."

Ariston grinned down at her, the happiness in his expression arresting. "Had I taken his initial price, at best he would have been offended. At worst he would have considered me a rube."

She laughed at her husband's prioritizing. She couldn't help herself.

"You really believe he would have been offended if you hadn't tried to talk him down that last *twenty* dollars?" She didn't buy it.

"That was just for fun. Did you not see how much he enjoyed the exchange?"

"You both enjoyed it too much."

"No indeed. It was just enough." He leaned down and kissed her forehead, the affectionate tenderness of the action going straight to her heart. "Now you have a memory to put with the carpet every time you walk in our foyer."

"Watch out, someone is going to think you are a closet romantic, Ariston." Someone like his wife.

"I am sure my reputation can handle it."

"If you say so."

"I do. The carpet you purchased for me on our first honeymoon—"

"With a lot less haggling," she interjected.

"You paid too much, but I did not mind."

"Oh, really?"

"Really."

"What about it?" she asked when he said nothing further as they meandered back toward the cruise dock.

"Hmm?"

"The carpet in your office—you were saying something about it when I interrupted you."

"Oh, yes. Only that it has brought a smile to my face on many occasions."

"Honestly?"

"Yes."

"Because you think I paid too much?" And he found that amusing?

"Because it reminds me of your very generous nature. Do you remember how you asked the merchant, who happened to be father and uncle to the women who made it, if you could give him money to pass directly onto the weavers in thanks for their skill and efforts?"

Honestly, she'd forgotten. "He was really pleased," she remembered.

"Yes. As I'm sure the women were as well to receive the money."

"So? That makes you smile, to think of that?" she clarified.

"Yes. Thoughts of you often make me smile."

"If you don't watch it, I'm going to think you've fallen for me."

He didn't look the least worried by the idea. "It is only natural that I should enjoy thoughts of my wife."

"Way to sidestep the issue."

He stopped in the street and looked down at her, his azure eyes probing. "Is there an issue?"

"No."

"You are happy?"

"Very much so." He made her feel like the most important woman in the world and how could she be anything less than thrilled with that?

Maybe words weren't as important as actions. She'd still like them—those three very important words that said so much—but wasn't about to live the rest of her life pining for something she might never have.

Enjoying what she *did* have sounded so much smarter.

# CHAPTER THIRTEEN

"WOULD you like to go swimming tonight?" Ariston asked as they entered their suite later to get ready for dinner. "We can take advantage of the privacy after the spa pool has been closed to the rest of the ship."

"Yes…" Chloe's voice trailed off, her eyes going wide at the changes in their room.

The table had been set elegantly for dinner, complete with white linens, LED candlelight and roses. Champagne chilled in a standing ice bucket beside it and a flat gift box rested on top of one of the place settings.

The bed had been turned down, rose petals strewn across its expanse, and chocolate truffles placed in the center of each of their pillows.

"What's going on? We're dining in tonight?"

"I hope you do not mind. It is our last night onboard. I wanted to spend it with you alone."

"You really *are* a closet romantic," she said with awe and just a touch of amusement.

He shrugged, but color burnished his cheekbones. "I ordered the honeymoon package. It is always good to check the quality of our services."

Right. Likely story. "So, it's all your ship's staff's fault?"

"You don't like it?"

"Don't be a jerk. I love it."

He moved to stand near her, reaching out to brush at the hair that had escaped the clip she'd put it in that morning. "First an idiot, now a jerk…I am worried what will come next."

"Man, you don't forget anything, do you?"

"No."

"I'll have to make sure I remember that."

"So, you are okay with having our last dinner onboard in our suite?"

"More than." She loved the idea of having him all to herself.

They would be returning to real life fast enough where his company demanded most of his waking hours.

"Good." He pulled her into his arms, his hands sliding down to press her body into his. "I enjoy having you to myself."

"Me too," she had no problem admitting.

They kissed, but he kept things from getting too intense. She didn't mind. There were a thousand different ways to kiss her husband and she enjoyed them all. This warm affirmation of affection was wonderful and she let herself melt into him, trusting that he would take care of them both.

After too short of the blissful interval, he pulled back. "Appetizers will be arriving momentarily."

"I'm going to be halfway to my weight goal for being able to get pregnant by the end of this cruise. You realize that, don't you?"

"I would like nothing better."

Only he didn't sound as if he was thinking about her weight at all. And for once, she didn't think the worst— like to wonder if the whole point of the honeymoon had been to get her ready for carrying his child. He'd been too attentive and consistent for her to think his motives for this trip had been mercenary.

She had a hard time attributing ulterior motives to anything he did when he made her feel so cherished.

She grinned. "Okay. Shall I dress for dinner?"

"It would be my preference that you undress, but since the wait staff will be delivering our food, I will be content if you stay as you are until then."

"I'm not eating in the nude, Ariston."

"Perhaps you would wear that lovely gown you bought in the gift shop?" he asked with a very hopeful expression.

"I didn't think you saw me buying that." It was a mint-green silk negligee complete with peignoir that she'd thought to surprise him with upon returning home.

And so she told him.

"You can surprise me again. Rest assured, my enthusiasm will not be dimmed for the repeated experience."

She nodded, thinking that maybe, like with the rug, having a nightgown that reminded him of the closeness and intimacy they'd shared on this trip would be a good thing.

"If I'm going to wear lingerie to dinner, I think I'll bathe beforehand. You can knock on the en suite after our food has been delivered." With that, she disappeared into the luxurious bathroom.

She'd thought cruise ship accommodations would be tighter, and no doubt they were in the rest of the ship, but Ariston's personal suite was spacious and had all the finer appointments, like leather furniture, a king-size bed that gave an absolutely fabulous night's rest and marble in the bathroom that came complete with a Jacuzzi tub.

She imagined all his top-of-the-line suites shared some things in common, but doubted any of them were quite as posh.

Chloe heard voices in the room after she'd been soaking only a few minutes. No wonder Ariston had been so careful to keep their kisses from going incendiary.

As much as she might have liked to relax in the tub longer, she made quick work of washing before letting the tub drain. It would have been more fun with Ariston anyway, and she didn't want to make dinner cold waiting on her.

She took only a few moments to lotion her face before brushing out her hair and donning the gorgeous nightgown and peignoir. The green silk was too thin to be completely opaque, but the lace-accented peignoir lent another layer of modesty...or titillation, depending on how one looked at it.

Her guess was that Ariston would lean toward the latter.

When she came out of the en suite, his expression was everything she could have wanted it to be upon seeing her. He looked as if he wanted to eat her up.

Perhaps she should have bought the matching set in white, only she'd thought it was too virginal and having been married twice now—if to the same man—she felt anything but.

"You'll have to wait until after dinner." She smiled, doing nothing to hide her own desire.

He crossed the room in a few long strides and pulled her against him. "Perhaps we should have dessert first."

"Anticipation will only improve the experience, or so you used to tell me." He hadn't made any such claims on this trip.

"I am less patient than I used to be, I find."

"Isn't it supposed to go the other way round? You're supposed to be more patient as you get older?" she teased.

"So Pappous says, but at least in this, I will have to believe he is wrong."

She shook her head, laughing softly as she pulled from Ariston's arms and went over to the table. "Dinner first. I didn't put this on just for you to take it right back off."

"But didn't the saleslady tell you that was exactly the destiny of such nightwear?"

She *had* actually and Chloe had blushed crimson. Now she just felt warm inside.

When she simply stood by the table expectantly, Ariston finally sighed, doing his best to look put-upon, but not succeeding with any real potency.

"Come, this is your seat." He pulled out the chair in front of the place setting with the gift.

"I thought maybe it was."

"Smart aleck."

"I like *yineka mou* better."

"I do too," he said in a strangely husky tone as he saw her seated.

She looked up, only to be caught by an intense azure gaze. No words passed between them for long moments as they maintained the electric eye contact.

Finally, he brushed his hand down her cheek. "Mine."

"For a lifetime, or so the paper says."

He nodded, not even cracking part of a smile at her attempt at humor. "So the paper says and this time, I will not let you go."

She couldn't help but believe him and that belief sent warmth unfurling through her heart.

"I'm not letting you go either," she promised.

"Good."

Once he'd found his own chair, she lifted the gift. "Am I to wait to open it?"

"I could say anticipation will make it all the better."

"You could." She tried to pretend it didn't matter, but they both knew she had a weakness for presents.

Always had.

"But I will not. Please, open it now."

She did so with alacrity, tearing at the heavyweight

embossed paper, but wasn't sure she understood what she found in the nicely wrapped box.

"This gallery is in New York, isn't it?" She held up a set of glossy photos of a nice-looking small gallery that seemed to display an eclectic assortment of artwork. "Are we going to an opening?"

She grinned before he could answer. "I would love that. You know how much I enjoy galleries that don't limit their pieces to one artistic genre."

"I am sure we will attend many openings at this particular gallery. Look at the papers below the pictures."

She lifted them out and unfolded what turned out to be an official-looking set of documents. "This is a deed," she whispered.

"Yes."

"In my name."

"It is."

"You bought me an art gallery?" She couldn't quite believe that's what all this meant. "In New York?"

"The first time you married me, you gave up your schooling. I cannot change that, though if you would like to enroll in the Art Institute of New York, I've had Jean confirm that your credits will transfer from the art institute you attended previously."

"Really? I…. That's great." She didn't know what else to say. She had no intention of going back to school, but she sensed that right now wasn't the time to get into that.

"This time, you had to give up personally running your gallery and shop in Oregon, the life you had built for yourself there. If I said I was sorry, I would be lying, because I want you with me, but I prefer you be happy in your new life. Not merely content."

"I see." Well, she didn't, not really, but it was amazing and wonderful and she would take it. She would so take it.

"You enjoyed running your gallery and shop on the coast. It is important you have something to occupy your passion for the arts in New York as well. You will have to have a proficient assistant manager as our life is not static and you will spend significant time away from New York though."

He sounded almost apologetic for that fact, but she didn't want him to be. This was amazing.

"That's fabulous!" She jumped up and was around the table in record time.

"You're wonderful!" Throwing herself into his lap, she kissed every inch of his face and neck that she could reach. "Thank you, Ariston. Thank you so much. I love it! This is the best gift anyone has ever given me. No one in my life has ever been so thoughtful."

"I could hardly get you a rug to put in your studio. It would be covered in paint splatters in no time," he said, sounding almost humble.

She knew better and she loved him for it. "You are the best husband ever."

And light-years ahead of her father, who had been happy enough for her mother to paint, but who had always made it clear that her mother's responsibilities as the wife to the owner of Dioletis Industries came first.

Ariston preened and grinned and then kissed her to within an inch of her life.

They didn't get to dinner until later after all.

When the ship docked the next morning, Ariston and Chloe disembarked and took one of the Spiridakou limousines to his grandfather's home outside Piraeus.

Takis had decided to make the most of his first trip to New York and had spent the first week of their trip allowing Chloe's father to show him around the Big Apple. He'd been home a couple of days now and had evinced excitement at their coming visit, when they'd called from the ship a couple of days before.

He made them sit on the terrace that overlooked the harbor and eat breakfast, sure they couldn't have had anything substantial before their early disembarkation. He was right, but not because breakfast wasn't available.

Chloe and Ariston had indeed gone swimming in the pool after hours and then he'd taken her back to their suite and made love to her until the wee hours of the morning. For the first time ever that Chloe knew about, Ariston had slept through his usual waking hour.

He and Chloe had barely woken in time to disembark the ship on schedule. Not that the staff wouldn't have made exceptions for the owner of the cruise line, but Ariston wasn't that kind of boss. He might be a billionaire tycoon and arrogant as all get-out, but he was a decent man.

And Chloe just loved him to death.

"What has you smiling?" Takis asked with his own grin.

She slid a glance at Ariston, who seemed preoccupied with the view, and just shook her head. "Nothing in particular. I'm just happy."

That had Ariston looking at her, his own expression softened.

Chloe told Takis about the gallery then, gushing over how wonderful a gift it was.

"I was surprised to hear you had decided to open a business rather than go back to school," Takis observed.

"It just worked out that way."

"Why? Surely with your divorce settlement..." Takis gave his grandson a look of definite censure. "You could have gone back to school and gotten your degree in fine arts."

"I thought about it, but I realized I had no desire to go

back to that world. I'd changed too much, I think. And while I truly love art, I don't have the passion as an artist to pursue that career. Nor do I have the talent," she admitted with self-deprecating honesty.

Both Ariston and Takis made noises as if to disagree and she smiled, but shook her head. "Don't. You two hung my paintings because I was family, not because of their artistic merit."

And it had shocked her to discover the watercolors she'd done for the breakfast room still hanging in the house in New York.

"That is not true," Takis said staunchly.

Ariston gave her a look probably meant to intimidate. "Even for family, I would not hang dreck on my walls."

She just smiled. "I didn't say they were dreck, just that I don't have the kind of brilliant talent it takes to be an artist of note. And I don't mind." She really, really didn't. "Accepting that I didn't mind is when I realized that I'd make a lousy artist. It's a career that takes deep and abiding passion. Mine was tied up elsewhere."

"Helping others pursue their dreams of sharing their art with the world," Ariston guessed.

He was half-right, so she nodded. "Yes. I'm not even sure now that I didn't attend art school in great part just to get as far away from *business* as I could. As it turned out, I really enjoyed running my art supply store and gallery."

It was her turn to look out over the harbor, the *Colossus* looking like a tiny white speck in the distance. "Providing the means and encouragement for budding artists to pursue their passion and established ones to display it for the world turned out to be more fulfilling than I would have thought possible. I didn't even mind doing the paperwork."

"That is a very laudable reason to run a business." No looks of reproof from Takis toward her.

"Thank you." She grimaced. "It's ironic that I ended up exactly where I'd been so determined not to though."

"Maybe not so much. You refused to be part of Dioletis Industries and that's what was of real importance to you," Takis suggested.

Ariston frowned and admitted, "I had thought you would take the divorce settlement and pour it back into the company."

"I'm sure my father would have been happier if I had." But Ariston knew now that would not have happened.

Ever.

"Perhaps. Perhaps he has learned his lesson." Takis's eyes glowed with a certain satisfaction.

Ariston glared at his grandfather. "You did not tell me you intended anything against Eber's company."

"I'm not a doddering old man. Just because I relinquished control of the company to you does not mean I need you approving my actions."

"I did not say it did." Affront radiated from Ariston.

Takis looked quite pleased with himself. "I may not run our company any longer, but I still have connections."

"I know you do." Now Ariston was sounding as if he wished he'd left the topic alone.

"Besides, it is not as if you did not have your own plans in that regard."

Chloe jerked around in her chair to look at Ariston in shock. "What's he talking about?"

Takis stood. "I will leave you two to talk."

"Thank you, Pappous," Ariston said, sounding anything but grateful.

Chloe was just confused. "I don't understand."

"The fact your father's company was on the brink of bankruptcy was not all down to his antiquated views on business."

"You're saying you engineered the downfall of Dioletis Industries?" she asked, shock coursing through her.

"With the help of your father's poor financial choices and my grandfather, though I did not know it, yes."

"Why?"

"It was necessary."

"To get revenge against me...or my father?"

Ariston had said he'd been livid about her not sticking to the intent of their contract. And he had to have been beyond furious that she'd walked out on him, though he'd never come right out and said so. But he'd never even hinted he'd been angry enough to bankrupt a company because of it.

"No."

She ignored his denial. "Was convincing me to marry you again part of your revenge plot? Once our children are born, are you going to manufacture evidence of my infidelity and take them from me?"

"Don't start imagining scenarios that have no basis in reality," he said on a teasing note.

"This isn't funny." She jumped up from the table, looking wildly around, but seeing no means of escape.

Oh, she could leave the terrace, but she couldn't run from what she'd heard.

"No, it is not. There. Is. No. Revenge. Plot." He spoke slowly, emphasizing each word.

But she wasn't having any of it. "Don't lie to me. You just as good as admitted to it and your grandfather was honest at least about punishing my father."

"Pappous had his own reasons for doing what he did. Mine were very different."

She wanted to believe him, but couldn't fathom how his words could be true. "What were they?"

"To bring you back into my bed, back into my life."

"You tore down a company just to get me back into your bed? That's insane."

"I do not do things on a small scale." He was still in his seat, but his entire body seemed to vibrate with tension. "And perhaps in the beginning, revenge played a role in what I wanted—but my revenge was not to hurt you. It was to get you back where you belonged. With me."

Could she believe him? "You're every bit as bad as my father. Maybe worse."

Ariston was up from the table faster than light and coming to her, putting his hands on her shoulders. "Do not say that. It is not true."

"Really? What would have happened to all those employees you used to manipulate me back into marriage if I had never come to you, if I'd refused?"

"I would have come to you, if I had to."

"And if I'd refused?"

"You weren't going to."

"You couldn't know that."

"You are here, aren't you?" he practically shouted. "I am no fool. I think my plans out carefully before taking action."

"But even you cannot predict every outcome. And let's be honest…if I'd refused, you wouldn't have been too broken up about the dissolution of Dioletis Industries."

"I would have been broken up all right." His tone was sincere, his expression grim.

"I don't understand," she admitted. If it really was all about getting her back… "Why not just come to Oregon and just ask me out?"

His arrested expression said the thought had not even occurred to him. Her brilliant business tycoon had overlooked the most obvious and easiest course of action. Why?

She stared up at him. "Does the word *overkill* mean anything to you?"

"I needed to be sure of my success."

"Why was it so important? Your grandfather," she guessed.

But even as much as Ariston cared for the old man, she still couldn't imagine him going to such lengths just to please him.

"No. It was not about Pappous, though I tried to tell myself he was my reason for needing to get you back so badly."

"He wasn't?" she asked, hope warring with terror at being disappointed again inside her.

"No."

"Why, then?"

"I was thirteen when my father divorced his third wife so he could marry a woman he claimed to love. That wife had been the most decent of all his conquests. She cared about my father, she cared about his family...Pappous... me. She tried to kill herself and I found her, blood all over the bathroom."

"Oh, Ariston. I'm so sorry."

He shook his head. "My father wasn't. He convinced her that he loved her and then when he got bored, he left. Like he always did...always will until even his money won't be able to pull in the beautiful women."

Chloe put her hands on Ariston's chest, trying to infuse him with comfort.

He closed his eyes, tilting his head back as if trying to hold in some great emotion. "I vowed then that I would never tell a woman falsely that I loved her."

"You told Shannon you loved her."

"And look what that got me. Humiliation and betrayal."

"I'm not Shannon and you aren't your father," Chloe pointed out with fear-spiked optimism.

He took in two deep breaths and let them out before dropping his head and opening his eyes, their cerulean depths filled with an emotion she was terrified to name lest she was wrong. "Saying it was not a positive experience for me."

"It can be." She smiled up at him, her eyes filled with tears. "I'll show you."

He shook his head. "I should go first. I am no weakling."

No, but he was a man who had been traumatized by the words. "I love you, Ariston. I never wanted to leave you in the first place and I never would have refused to come back. *I love you* and I always have."

"Why the birth control?" he asked starkly, as if the words came from somewhere deep inside him. "If you wanted to be with me, why make sure our marriage was doomed to failure?"

"I wanted you to love me before we had children together and were irrevocably linked."

"You wanted our marriage to be about emotion, not a contract." His tone was more subdued than she'd ever heard it.

"Yes, but that doesn't matter anymore. Regardless of what prompted our marriage, I love being your wife. You have to understand, Ariston, just being with you makes me happy."

"Being with you makes me happy too."

"Because?"

"Because I..." His voice choked off and he had to take another deep breath, his cerulean depths suspiciously shiny. "Because I love you. I do, more than I knew a man could love a woman. I can't stand the thought of you ever leaving me."

"I won't." She made it a vow from the very depth of her soul.

"I'm not like your father."

"In the important things, no, you aren't." And her father had shown that even men like him could change.

"I won't neglect you or our children for SSE. I have an excellent management team. I don't have to spend sixty hours a week at my office."

"I'm glad to hear that."

"I want children."

"I know."

"But not for Pappous. I want them for us, because I want a little girl with your eyes and little boy who wants to grow up to be a painter."

"Not a CEO?"

"Can't we have more than one?"

She laughed at that, the joy just spilling out of her. "Let's let the future take care of itself."

"I'm not very good at that."

"I'll teach you."

"You've already taught me the most important thing."

"How to say 'I love you'?"

"How *to* love."

Tears slipped down her own cheeks and she sniffed. "We have a lifetime to get it perfect."

"It already is."

"I never thought I'd hear you say you love me," Chloe admitted in wonder.

"I never thought I'd have the courage." That admission cost him, even as Ariston showed with his open expression that he didn't regret making it.

"I left two years ago because I thought you would never love me."

"Because of the divorce papers."

"That and the fact you never said the words."

"Pappous always told me they weren't necessary."

"I adore your grandfather, but he's not always right."

"Don't let him hear you say so."

"I won't."

"I love you," Ariston said again, pulling her even closer, as if trying to meld their bodies.

"I love you so much, Ariston. I have from the very beginning."

"That's what you hoped for," he realized with wonder. "My love."

"Yes."

"You have it. Forever."

"And always." Sappy tears burned her eyes, but she wasn't embarrassed.

Her mom would have approved.

Chloe would never regret having the courage to take a chance on love, even love that seemed hopeless.

"Our children will know love," Ariston said with great satisfaction.

"Oh, yes…both our love for them, but they will also witness our love for each other and feel safe because of it."

"It is good for a child to feel safe."

"And loved."

"And loved."

"You are mine, yesterday, today and always."

"And you are mine, Mr. Tycoon."

"Even tycoons need love."

"I always knew that."

"I didn't."

"But you were smart enough to learn."

"You taught me." Ariston's eyes grew suspiciously bright before he lowered his head and kissed her.

When the kiss ended, she was in his arms, cradled against his chest, their breathing labored with passion.

Their gazes locked. "Thank you," he said with so much emotion, Chloe's heart squeezed.

She tilted her head up until their lips met again just briefly. "Thank you, for overcoming your fear and loving me."

"I didn't have a choice."

She smiled and repeated something he had said to her weeks ago. "We all have choices."

"Some really are easier to make than others. Like loving you."

"Like loving you."

And then he took her to their room and proved once again just how easy and wonderful that particular choice was.

\* \* \* \* \*

# ROMANCE

| | |
|---|---|
| **Banished to the Harem** | Carol Marinelli |
| **Not Just the Greek's Wife** | Lucy Monroe |
| **A Delicious Deception** | Elizabeth Power |
| **Painted the Other Woman** | Julia James |
| **A Game of Vows** | Maisey Yates |
| **A Devil in Disguise** | Caitlin Crews |
| **Revelations of the Night Before** | Lynn Raye Harris |
| **Defying her Desert Duty** | Annie West |
| **The Wedding Must Go On** | Robyn Grady |
| **The Devil and the Deep** | Amy Andrews |
| **Taming the Brooding Cattleman** | Marion Lennox |
| **The Rancher's Unexpected Family** | Myrna Mackenzie |
| **Single Dad's Holiday Wedding** | Patricia Thayer |
| **Nanny for the Millionaire's Twins** | Susan Meier |
| **Truth-Or-Date.com** | Nina Harrington |
| **Wedding Date with Mr Wrong** | Nicola Marsh |
| **The Family Who Made Him Whole** | Jennifer Taylor |
| **The Doctor Meets Her Match** | Annie Claydon |

# MEDICAL

| | |
|---|---|
| **A Socialite's Christmas Wish** | Lucy Clark |
| **Redeeming Dr Riccardi** | Leah Martyn |
| **The Doctor's Lost-and-Found Heart** | Dianne Drake |
| **The Man Who Wouldn't Marry** | Tina Beckett |

# Mills & Boon® Large Print
## October 2012

# ROMANCE

| | |
|---|---|
| **A Secret Disgrace** | Penny Jordan |
| **The Dark Side of Desire** | Julia James |
| **The Forbidden Ferrara** | Sarah Morgan |
| **The Truth Behind his Touch** | Cathy Williams |
| **Plain Jane in the Spotlight** | Lucy Gordon |
| **Battle for the Soldier's Heart** | Cara Colter |
| **The Navy SEAL's Bride** | Soraya Lane |
| **My Greek Island Fling** | Nina Harrington |
| **Enemies at the Altar** | Melanie Milburne |
| **In the Italian's Sights** | Helen Brooks |
| **In Defiance of Duty** | Caitlin Crews |

# HISTORICAL

| | |
|---|---|
| **The Duchess Hunt** | Elizabeth Beacon |
| **Marriage of Mercy** | Carla Kelly |
| **Unbuttoning Miss Hardwick** | Deb Marlowe |
| **Chained to the Barbarian** | Carol Townend |
| **My Fair Concubine** | Jeannie Lin |

# MEDICAL

| | |
|---|---|
| **Georgie's Big Greek Wedding?** | Emily Forbes |
| **The Nurse's Not-So-Secret Scandal** | Wendy S. Marcus |
| **Dr Right All Along** | Joanna Neil |
| **Summer With A French Surgeon** | Margaret Barker |
| **Sydney Harbour Hospital: Tom's Redemption** | Fiona Lowe |
| **Doctor on Her Doorstep** | Annie Claydon |

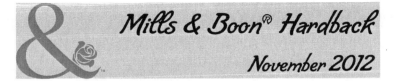

*Mills & Boon® Hardback*

*November 2012*

# ROMANCE

# MEDICAL

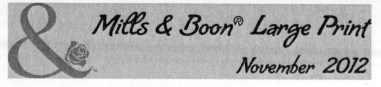

# Mills & Boon® Large Print
## November 2012

# ROMANCE

| | |
|---|---|
| **The Secrets She Carried** | Lynne Graham |
| **To Love, Honour and Betray** | Jennie Lucas |
| **Heart of a Desert Warrior** | Lucy Monroe |
| **Unnoticed and Untouched** | Lynn Raye Harris |
| **Argentinian in the Outback** | Margaret Way |
| **The Sheikh's Jewel** | Melissa James |
| **The Rebel Rancher** | Donna Alward |
| **Always the Best Man** | Fiona Harper |
| **A Royal World Apart** | Maisey Yates |
| **Distracted by her Virtue** | Maggie Cox |
| **The Count's Prize** | Christina Hollis |

# HISTORICAL

| | |
|---|---|
| **An Escapade and an Engagement** | Annie Burrows |
| **The Laird's Forbidden Lady** | Ann Lethbridge |
| **His Makeshift Wife** | Anne Ashley |
| **The Captain and the Wallflower** | Lyn Stone |
| **Tempted by the Highland Warrior** | Michelle Willingham |

# MEDICAL

| | |
|---|---|
| **Sydney Harbour Hospital: Lexi's Secret** | Melanie Milburne |
| **West Wing to Maternity Wing!** | Scarlet Wilson |
| **Diamond Ring for the Ice Queen** | Lucy Clark |
| **No.1 Dad in Texas** | Dianne Drake |
| **The Dangers of Dating Your Boss** | Sue MacKay |
| **The Doctor, His Daughter and Me** | Leonie Knight |

WEB/M&B/RTL3 HB

*Discover Pure Reading Pleasure with*

**Visit the Mills & Boon website for all
the latest in romance**

**Buy** all the latest releases, backlist and eBooks

**Find out** more about our authors and their books

**Join** our community and chat to authors and other readers

**Free** online reads from your favourite authors

**Win** with our fantastic online competitions

**Sign** up for our free monthly eNewsletter

**Tell us** what you think by signing up to our reader panel

**Rate** and review books with our star system

# www.millsandboon.co.uk

 Follow us at twitter.com/millsandboonuk

Become a fan at facebook.com/romancehq